More love stories by Amanda Hamm

LOVE IN ANDAUK
EVERYTHING OLD (BOOK 1)
INTO THE FIRE (BOOK 2)
BY ITS COVER (BOOK 3)
WHAT GOES AROUND (BOOK 4)

THEY SEE A FAMILY
THE STUDY GROUP (EBOOK NOVELLA)

COFFEE AND DONUTS
SAID AND UNSAID (BOOK 1)
SOFIE WAITS (BOOK 2)
A PERFECTLY GOOD MAN (BOOK 3)
NOT COMPLICATED (BOOK 4)

STORIES FROM HARTFORD
ANDREW'S KEY (BOOK 1)
JEALOUSY & YAMS (BOOK 2)
COLLECTING ZEBRAS (BOOK 3)
THE CHRISTMAS PROJECT (BOOK 4)
HEARTS ON THE WINDOW (EBOOK NOVELLA)

MEET CUTE: 5 ROMANTIC SHORT STORIES

THE 4TH FLOOR LOUNGE

The Art of Introductions

Romance Arts
Book 1

Amanda Hamm

ISBN: 978-1-943598-14-4

The Art of Introductions is a work of fiction. All names, characters, places, events, etc. are products of the author's imagination or are used fictitiously.

The sun glinted off the door as he opened it. Trevor Norman squinted against the visual intrusion. He was not a morning person. That bit of sun on the silver frame was enough to make him grumpy, or maybe grumpier. The boisterous laughter inside the January Café didn't help. It was too early for people to be so cheerful.

There was a group of older men at the back table, five or six of them. It was too early to count. Trevor knew there were five of them. There were always five of them, and he could see that without really counting. He liked the idea that it was too early to count.

The chairs along the counter had red and white striped vinyl that he thought his grandparents were a little nutty for choosing. They owned the place so they could do whatever nutty things they wanted. He took a seat in the closest chair with a wave at his grandpa – one of the loud men in the back – while he waited for his grandma to pop out of the kitchen. They both considered themselves retired and only came in for a few hours to open the restaurant, as though getting out before breakfast was a hobby. A manager came in later to run the place the rest of the day.

"Look what the cat dragged in," Grandma May said as she emerged. "It's my favorite grandchild." She smiled brightly at him.

The familiar greeting put a chink in Trevor's dark mood. He almost smiled back. The woman had nine grandchildren and called them all her favorite.

"You look extra grouchy so this probably isn't a good morning to tell you this." She rested her forearm on the counter and leaned on it. "Coffee maker's on the fritz."

Trevor didn't understand. He looked again at his grandpa and his friends. They all had mugs. One of them was drinking from his. Surely that was coffee. "On the fritz how?" he asked.

"Don't know," she said. "It's just not making coffee."

"They have coffee." He nodded to the back table.

"Yeah, it made one pot before it quit. Grandpa Paul will take a look at it when he's done flapping his jaws." She sent an affectionate glance that way before she turned back to Trevor.

"You're saying you don't have any for me?"

She threw her head back and laughed. "Now he's catching on! The slow uptake probably means you need it."

"The coffee you don't have?"

"Yep." Grandma May's smile appeared generally joyful and not at Trevor's expense.

That was good because the predicament was her fault. He'd made a habit of stopping in to say hello since he got a job down the street two years ago. At some point, she'd started serving him a cup of coffee as an excuse to linger. At some slightly later point, the coffee had become almost as important to him as the visit.

"Well... are you, uh..." She'd said something yesterday that he'd intended to ask about. What was it?

"Did the storm wake you up last night?"

He shook his head. He hadn't heard anything, and it didn't even look wet outside.

"Passed through pretty quickly," she said, "but the thunder woke me up sometime after midnight. Loud."

"I didn't hear anything."

"Slept through a lot more when I was young, too." She smiled sympathetically and tipped her head to the side. "Why don't you run over to the antique shop next door?"

Trevor wrinkled his eyebrows at her. He didn't think it was only his sluggish brain that made that suggestion out-of-the-blue and weird. "Do you need something?"

"You do," she said. "They have coffee over there. Grab yourself a cup so you can wake up before our visiting time is over."

Trevor stared at his grandmother, trying to process the information. He hadn't paid much attention to the business on the other side. Antiques and coffee didn't seem to go together though.

"Go on now." She patted his arm with one hand and made a shooing motion with the other.

He sighed and got up to follow her directions. Back on the street, he looked up at the sign on the next building. Next Love. That name didn't really say antiques or coffee. There were a couple of wooden dressers displayed in the window. One had little white flowers painted on the handles. The entrance was a fancy wooden door with a semicircle of etched glass. There was an open sign next to it so Trevor grabbed the handle and pulled.

The door was lighter than he expected. He stumbled and held on until he got his footing again. Apparently, it was too early to successfully operate a door. Although, he was inside. Perhaps that counted as success.

The place had an aisle straight up the center to another door at the back. Trevor had a fleeting thought of gratitude that he didn't have to attempt that one. He'd had enough doors. Both sides of the room were crammed with mostly wooden furniture of various types. But he did smell coffee. Where was that smell coming from?

There was a woman nearby who turned towards him when he entered. She had wavy shoulder-length hair that was mostly dark gray with some brownish strands mixed in. She looked sixtyish. A steaming mug was cradled between her hands.

"Good morning!" Her smile was welcoming, but before he could ask if she worked there, she added, "She'll help you," with a nod deeper into the store.

Trevor caught the eye of another woman. She appeared around the same age and was opening and closing the drawers of a dresser as tall as she was. She had only glanced over, and she immediately returned her focus to the drawers. It seemed she had no intention of doing anything else.

"Red shirt." The closer woman took one hand off the mug to point.

There was a third person, also female, near the back of the store. She was wearing a red shirt so Trevor began to walk towards her. He was beginning to feel he was on a bizarre scavenger hunt for coffee. Find one grandma, one fancy door, two unhelpful women and another one... sanding a table? Sand was definitely not an ingredient in coffee. He approached her anyway. The woman in the red shirt had her back to him. She moved a sanding block in small circles along the edge of a dining table while her long brown ponytail swayed side to side.

"Excuse me," he said.

The sander flipped out of her hand onto the table. He'd clearly startled her. She turned around. This woman was much younger than the first two. And prettier. And his mind went completely blank except for the appreciation of the contours of her face. Her hand came up to rub the back of her nose with her wrist. One eyebrow twitched. "Can I help you?" she asked.

Her voice was pretty, too. It was soft but not quiet. "Yes," he said. He would like her help.

Eyelids dropped over eyes the color of coffee in a slow blink. She blinked again. "*How* can I help you?"

That was a fascinating question. If he was a little more alert, he could probably think of a lot of ways. A thought was trying to make its way from the back of his head about something specific. He noticed her eye color again. "Oh… I, uh, I heard there was coffee here."

"Sure. I'll get you a cup." She looked at her hands. "Just give me a minute to clean up."

As she walked away, Trevor became aware that he no longer smelled coffee in this part of the shop. The scent in the air was wood and paint and nothing related to food. The young woman quickly disappeared into a restroom. He just stood where she'd left him. Two minutes later, she popped back out and held up a finger as a command to continue waiting. Then she disappeared through that large door at the back.

"She forgot to ask if you wanted anything in it."

The voice made him jump. Trevor realized the first woman was standing at his elbow. She was still holding the mug with both hands but because he was taller, he could see coffee filled only a quarter of the mug.

"She'll remember," she said with a nod. She seemed to be talking to herself. That impression was heightened by the fact that she moved away again without waiting for a response.

The younger woman returned holding a styrofoam cup. She got within a few feet before she addressed Trevor. "I forgot to ask if you want anything in it. We don't have anything fancy, just milk or sugar."

"I usually have a spoon of sugar," he said.

She spun around with that lovely ponytail swinging.

Trevor's hand twitched with a pathetic and belated attempt to take the cup. He'd been about to add that he could just have it plain today so he wouldn't put her to more trouble. But she reset her path so fast that stopping her seemed like more trouble.

When she finally passed him the cup, she held it an extra second to make sure he had a good grip. Perhaps she noticed that he was distracted by the eyes watching him take it. He quickly took a sip to show his gratitude. It was too hot to get a good taste, and the roof of his mouth was scalded. That woke him up enough to remember a better way to show gratitude. "Thank you," he said.

She nodded. "Is there anything else I can help you with?"

Trevor wasn't in a hurry for her to leave, and he'd been standing there long enough to be curious about his surroundings. He mumbled the store name that still meant nothing to him. "What is this place?" he asked.

"We sell second-hand furniture."

"Like a perpetual garage sale?" The items around him were scratched and faded and old. It all looked like a big garage sale.

"No," she said, somewhat defensively. "We fix it up first."

"This junk doesn't look fixed up." He took a more careful drink of the coffee. It was good.

She paused before she answered. The irritation in her eyes suggested she wasn't giving him a chance to enjoy the flavor. "It isn't. We do custom work."

"What do you mean?"

"All right." She pointed to the front of the store. "We keep a few finished things up by the window as samples. Most of the items in the showroom have been repaired where necessary... new hinges, drawer guides, that sort of thing. But we haven't done anything cosmetic. That way people can choose a stain that matches what they already have or a design for a specific theme. We do a lot of pieces for kids' rooms with names painted on them."

Trevor was listening. It sounded like an interesting business. He wanted to learn more. As he looked around, however, he saw the woman with the mug that must be empty by now leaning against a wall staring at them. He turned so that he wasn't facing her. "What's with your creepy coworker?"

She narrowed her eyes in confusion. "I don't... what are you talking about?"

"The woman staring at us," he said. "When I came in, she sent me to you even though she wasn't doing anything. Lazy and creepy, apparently."

Her eyes moved before she smiled and then waved at the coworker. "That's…" She stopped and seemed to change her mind about what she was going to say. "That's not terribly surprising."

"The lazy part or the creepy part?"

"Um…" She pressed her lips against a smile. "Both, I guess. Are you shopping at all today?"

"What, here?"

"No. The other store you walked into." Her sarcasm was delivered with a smile.

Trevor had finished about half the coffee, but the caffeine hadn't kicked in yet. He was vaguely aware that the smile might be generous. "I don't think I need any furniture."

"You don't think?" she asked. "Would you like to look around a bit?"

"Look around for what I don't need?" He gave a short laugh. "You sound like a salesman."

"I… am a salesman." She spread her arms to indicate their surroundings.

It brought his attention to the table she'd been working on when he came in. "What are you doing with that table?"

She glanced over her shoulder, then back at him. "The one I'm sanding?"

"Yeah. Are you selling that?"

"Not anymore."

"Huh?"

"This one is already sold," she said.

"Oh, right." Trevor nodded as he remembered. "You clean things up after you sell them."

"Everything here is *clean*."

He paused, trying not to be annoyed that she seemed to be willfully misunderstanding him. "I meant clean it up in the sense of... the appearance, improving the general appearance."

"I know." She offered a faint smile.

That was all the apology he needed. Her smile, even the hint of it, was fairly mesmerizing. He stared at her mouth as it faded away. Then her eyes widened in an unspoken question. It looked as though she was asking if he was done talking to her. Trevor did not want to be done. "So what are you doing to that table?"

"I'm sanding it."

"I see that," he said. Although he was the one who had asked a question with an obvious answer. Twice.

She dipped her head in concession and took a step closer to the table with a gesture for him to follow. "I've already removed the old scratched finish with a power sander, but I like to do a final pass by hand." She glanced up to see if he understood so far.

He nodded at her.

"Okay. Once I'm sure it's smooth, I'll redo the finish to match... hang on a second." She moved away. There was a counter with a cash register nearby. She reached under it to pull out a phone. She was tapping and swiping as she returned. "The woman who ordered it," she said, "has a curio cabinet in her dining room that... here it is." She turned the phone around so that Trevor could see a picture of a cabinet with several panes of glass on the front.

He studied it a moment though he wasn't entirely sure what he was looking at, or why.

"We're going to make the table the same color and..." She turned the phone around and zoomed in before she turned it back to him. "See the black swirls on the wood between the panes? She wants us to copy that design along the beveled edge of the table."

"You can do that?"

"Oh, copying is easy." She stuck the phone in her back pocket. "You know those pictures in like kids' magazines where there's a grid behind it and you draw the different sections?"

"I think so," he said. "I've never done one of those because they look kind of dumb."

"Well... I do something like that to copy a design or picture. The difficult orders are when a customer only describes something, and then we have to translate that into a picture."

"Hmm. How long will this take?"

"I, uh... It's hard to say. Sometimes it depends how much I get interrupted."

She seemed to be hinting at something, and Trevor had had enough coffee to understand that he was interrupting her. "I guess I should leave you to your work." He wiggled his empty cup. "I don't see a trash can."

"I'll take that." She held out her hand.

He tried to give her the cup, but he somehow botched the handoff. The cup jumped over her hand and flipped across the table. A worried expression covered her face only a second before she lunged forward to grab the cup with one hand. At the same time, her other hand used the bottom of her shirt to wipe away a few drips before they could soak into the wood. She frowned at the table, casting her eyes over it for anything she might have missed.

Trevor stood there marveling at how quick and graceful her movements were. She'd snatched up the cup before it'd stopped bouncing and before he'd had much chance to react. His only reaction had been to kick himself for being klutzy. It hadn't occurred to him that her table might need rescuing from remnants of liquid until she'd already done it. "Sorry about that," he said.

"It's okay." Her words sounded like a reflex. Then she turned her eyes from the table and smiled that pretty smile again. "Better now than after I've finished it, right?"

"Uh, yeah. Thanks again for the coffee." Trevor moved towards the exit before he could do any more damage. That woman with the empty mug was still holding it with both hands, still leaning against a wall. She watched him walk out looking oddly satisfied. He got a glimpse of her rushing towards the back as the door closed behind him.

2

$\mathcal{T}$ he sun was in his eyes as he opened the door again. Who put that annoying silver frame on there anyway? Grandpa Paul's voice was the first one he heard, telling a familiar joke to his friends. They were guffawing before he even got to the punchline. Trevor tried not to roll his tired eyes as he held a hand up in greeting.

"Trevor!" Grandpa Paul called to him from halfway across the restaurant. "Get in here and say hello to your grandmother. She was worried when you disappeared yesterday."

He hadn't disappeared. She'd sent him away. But he went over and sat at the counter without arguing.

Grandma May came out of the kitchen wearing a smile way too bright for morning. "Look what the cat dragged in," she said. "It's my favorite grandchild."

Trevor made a half-hearted attempt to return her smile. It was too early to smile.

"You look as grouchy as usual so I hate to have to tell you this." She set an empty coffee pot on the counter next to him. "Coffee maker's on the fritz again."

He smelled coffee. Someone nearby had coffee. He looked in disbelief at the drips in the bottom of the pot. "Don't tell me it made one pot and quit again."

"Yep." She somehow looked apologetic and amused at the same time. "How'd you guess?"

"I think it might be Groundhog Day," he said.

She laughed heartily at his joke, which was somehow annoying. It was apparently too early for jokes. "How are you feeling this morning?" he asked.

"Nothing to complain about."

Trevor only nodded. He'd meant to follow up on an aching shoulder she'd mentioned yesterday. But he was suddenly less sure it was yesterday. It might have been three or four days already. His show of concern would sound pathetic when coupled with lateness. He stared into the empty coffee pot as he tried to think of something else to ask.

"How are the boys in your weekly card club?" she asked first.

"It's not a card club."

"Audra calls it the card club."

"Yeah, well, Audra is…" He couldn't think of a polite way to insult his sister in front of his grandmother. "Wrong," he finished.

"Was there a Logan and Cameron are fine in there?"

"Huh?"

"Oh, Trevor, you…" She kept shaking her head but cut off her words as she looked up to see who was coming into the restaurant. "Morning, Myra." Grandma May held up the empty pot.

"Again? What kind of two-bit establishment are you running here?"

Trevor recognized the name and the voice that carried across the space as his great aunt, his grandma's sister. Several of the men yelled greetings to her as well. Trevor put a hand on his forehead as he wondered why all the old people in his life were so loud. Weren't these people supposed to teach him how to have conversations with inside voices?

Myra plunked herself at the counter next to Trevor and addressed her sister in a voice loud enough for everyone to hear. "Shouldn't you get your lazy husband to work on that coffee pot?"

"Pot's fine," Grandpa Paul called. "It's the percolator that needs help... perking."

"I take it back," Myra said. "I'm not sure he should be working on anything."

"Someone should." Grandma May patted Trevor's arm. "My favorite grandchild isn't going to make it through the day without some caffeine."

Trevor raised his head from his hand. "I'll be fine." He would wake up eventually. It would just take longer without the pick-me-up.

"Did you have any trouble getting coffee at the antique store yesterday?" she asked.

"Getting coffee? No."

Concern appeared on her face. "Was there another problem?"

He shook his head. She shouldn't waste energy on concern. He was the one who'd embarrassed himself many times over. Some of it was kind of a blur at the moment, but he remembered spending a lot of the afternoon cringing.

"I guess I can look at it now." Grandpa Paul stood up with an exaggerated groan and an odd glance at his wife. Odd because he seemed to be checking for permission.

A couple of his friends began to berate him.

"You think you can teach that old thing some new tricks?"

"Try not to electrocute yourself."

"It was a couple of sparks," he said to much laughter.

"He's going to be awhile even once he gets started." Grandma May leaned closer to Trevor and spoke in her normal voice as though it was a whisper. "You should head next door for your coffee."

He shouldn't. He really shouldn't. Trevor nodded anyway. "Have a nice day, Grandma. You, too, Aunt Myra." He raised a hand to the group of old men. They were now engaged in a somewhat scary discussion about when it was necessary to shut off the circuit breaker. Most of them still nodded or waved in response.

Standing on the sidewalk, Trevor tried to wake himself up before he entered Next Love. Squinting in the sun made him want to close his eyes altogether though, and that wasn't helping. He put his hand on the handle of the fancy door. Again it came at him more easily than expected. He didn't stumble, but he nearly smacked himself in the face with it. What was wrong with that door?

The wood and chemical smell was already familiar. Trevor glanced around hopefully, but he didn't see her. There were a few people who appeared to be browsing the furniture. An older woman was headed towards him, older but probably closer to his mom's age than his grandmother's. Instead of gray and brown hair, this one had yellowy blonde hair that did not look natural. She was holding a coffee mug between her hands just like the woman who greeted him the previous day though, and he wondered if it could be the same woman. He really wasn't sure.

"Good morning!" She smiled and moved one hand in what seemed like a welcoming gesture. He could see now that her cup was empty, like his grandmother's pot.

"Good morning," he said. "I'm looking for coffee."

She nodded. "You can ask Alison."

He could. If he had any idea who Alison was. He hoped she was the woman who had been wearing a red shirt yesterday, but he still didn't see her anywhere.

"She's working on something in the back," said the woman gripping her mug. "You'll find her if you head that way." Her tone was certain and conveyed the expectation that it was all the help Trevor needed and therefore all he was going to get.

He walked down the open area in the center of the shop scanning the spaces between tables and cabinets and... jewelry? There was one cabinet with its doors open. The inside was covered with nails, from which hung various pieces of beaded jewelry. They had individual price tags and were so sparkly they seemed out of place among all the scuffed furniture. That was something he could ask Alison about if she was whom he hoped she was, and if he could find her.

He'd nearly made it to the back door when he was startled to see a woman sitting on the floor. She was hidden behind a large armoire so he didn't see her until she was a few feet away. Her back was towards him again, but he recognized the long brown ponytail. It was tied with a shiny blue ribbon. With her stained jeans and gray t-shirt, it seemed about as out-of-place as the sparkly jewelry.

Yet it also seemed just right. There was an end table with two small doors open in front of her and a bunch of hinges spread out on the floor. She must have sensed someone close because she looked up. "Oh, hi. Can I help you?"

"Yes." He fought through the grogginess in his brain to get to the most important part. "You gave me some coffee yesterday, and I was so out of it I didn't realize until sometime after I left that I hadn't paid for it."

"Oh, that's…" She shook her head and seemed to be looking for words. "We don't charge for coffee," she said after a moment. "It's just something we offer to customers in the morning so no one is drinking it in front of them."

He was relieved there was no charge. At least he hadn't done anything literally criminal. "Could I possibly trouble you for another cup today?"

"Sure." She pushed the hinges away to give herself room to stand. "Be right back."

She was already out of sight when Trevor thought he could have offered her a hand. He was kind of glad he hadn't. She got up so fast she clearly didn't need the help so she might have thought he was only trying to hold her hand for a minute. Probably not. It was always too early to try to guess what a pretty woman might be thinking.

He squatted to examine the hinges she'd left. He'd seen hinges before of course but not some that weren't attached to anything. Some of them fell open or closed when he picked them up. Some were tighter and needed some force to move. Then he pinched his finger in one.

He pulled his hand back as he noticed the woman returning with his coffee. She was close enough that she had to have seen him messing with her stuff. And hurting himself with it. Stupid. He stood up and reached for the cup. "Thank you. Is your name Alison, by the way?"

"Yeah." She looked surprised and, more importantly, distracted from him playing with hinges.

He waved towards the front of the shop. "The woman with the weird hair told me to ask Alison about coffee. I took a guess that was you."

"Weird hair?" Her eyes were wide, more in question than shock. He hoped.

Trevor was kicking himself for saying that out loud. He took a drink, trying to trigger a filter. "I mean, um…" The woman in question was leaning against a wall with her empty mug, watching just as the day before. "Is that the same woman who was here yesterday?"

"The creepy, lazy woman?"

It seemed Alison had a good memory. That could be a serious problem. "The one who… uh… Do you have more than one coworker who walks around with a white coffee mug?"

"No. She dyed her hair yesterday evening." Alison flicked her eyes to the older woman and back. "Do you not like it?"

"I didn't say that," Trevor said. He searched his sleepy brain for confirmation. He was mostly sure he hadn't said that. Repeating that he'd only said it was weird would probably not improve his defense. "I only meant that it was… different… than yesterday."

Alison laughed and said, "Relax. I'm just giving you a hard time."

Trevor still wanted to change the subject. He pointed to the hinges. "What are you doing this morning?"

"I'm trying to find some matching hinges."

"For the little cabinet?"

"Uh-huh."

"It has hinges," he said.

"I know. The woman who's buying it wants us to at least try to get four the same."

Trevor examined the inside. The hinges already looked the same to him.

"The metal on the left is darker," Alison explained. Because she could tell he didn't see a difference.

He still didn't, but he nodded anyway. "Why?"

"We thought it'd be close enough."

"Oh." Trevor tried not to show how confused he was. "You put the hinges on, and now you're putting on different ones?"

She nodded. "Do you really want to hear about it?"

"Yes."

"Well, reusing stuff is kind of our thing," she said. "We're trying to give all this furniture new life, and the parts. Whenever we take off a hinge or a handle or something, we save it in case it will work on another piece."

"But why do you take it off if it's still good?"

"Lots of reasons. Sometimes we might buy an old dresser with, like, four drawers where one of them is missing a handle so we'll replace all of them to match and save the three we took off for something with fewer drawers. Or sometimes a knob or handle will be loose and we'll want something with a different shape to cover where we had to drill a new hole or patch something to secure it. And sometimes the customer just doesn't like the handles on it."

"Same with the hinges?" he asked.

"Yeah. Since those are usually hidden on the inside, we don't worry as much about making an exact match. Functional is more important. In this case," she pointed to the little cabinet with its doors open, "we put, um… I don't remember which side we replaced, but it was missing one hinge so we replaced both on that side even though they were slightly lighter or darker than the other. They're covered up when the doors are closed, and you can't tell if only one door is open or even in poor lighting."

Trevor still couldn't see a difference between the two sides. Maybe the doors were casting shadows from his perspective. He might be able to tell if he got closer, but he didn't want to be obvious about trying to get a better look. He simply nodded and continued to take her word for it. "That's not good enough for someone?"

Alison shrugged. "Well, it is, and it isn't. She's going to buy it even if we can't find four the same, but she asked if we'd make an effort. I think this has been in our inventory long enough that our hinge supply is different than when we looked before so this is me making an effort."

"If you find one, are you… You're saying *we* a lot. Will you be the one who actually replaces the hinges?"

"Yeah."

"I'm impressed."

She dropped her eyes to the cabinet and back up. "You're impressed that I can use a screwdriver?"

"No. I… um…" What had he meant? He'd never replaced a hinge, but apparently, it was easy.

"How's the coffee?"

Trevor jumped at the voice behind him even though he kind of wanted to hug the creepy woman for her timely interruption. "It's very good. Thank you."

"I knew Alison would take care of you," she said. "You go ahead and ask any question at all." Empty mug woman moved away holding a meaningful look with Alison.

Trevor did not understand the meaning. When he turned back to Alison, her hair ribbon caught his eye and reminded him there was a question he wanted to ask. "I noticed a cabinet full of jewelry over there."

Her eyes darted that way. "Did you want to buy something?"

"Oh, no, I..." He clamped his mouth shut before he said something unintentionally insulting about the jewelry. He'd felt an impulse to make clear that he had no one to give jewelry to, but he didn't want to imply there was anything wrong with it. The gears of his brain were getting less sticky, and he tried to weed out any unnecessary words. He could ask a simple question. "What is it?" he said.

Alison got a weird look on her face, like she was confused and trying not to laugh. "The... jewelry?"

He just told her he saw some jewelry and then asked what it was. In trying to make sure he didn't call it odd or out-of-place, he didn't call it anything. "I'm curious about the jewelry because it's not furniture."

"It's jewelry," she said. There was something in her eyes that suggested she was enjoying the repetition.

"Is it... for sale?"

She smiled.

He'd already said he didn't want to buy any and now was asking if it was for sale. This was more of a useless circle than an intelligent conversation.

Alison began to explain. "I know the jewelry stands out. It's made by a local woman, an old friend of my mom's actually, who approached us about displaying some of her work. She also has an online store and apparently does fairly well."

"So you sort of rent her space?"

"Yeah. She comes in every few weeks to check her inventory and collect what we've sold," Alison said. "It's a fairly informal arrangement."

"What about the thing displaying the jewelry?"

"The armoire?"

He knew what it was, but he didn't blame her for thinking that was his question. "I mean, can you still sell that with all the nail holes in it?"

"We probably could because we're good." Alison paused to wink. "But it belongs to Sheila, the woman who makes the jewelry. She bought it to have a display that blends in."

Trevor nodded at what sounded like a very practical idea, to buy a display case already there rather than bring one in. He ran a hand over a rough spot on one side as he realized he and Alison had walked closer to the case while they talked.

"I can take the cup if you're done with it," Alison offered.

He hadn't finished, but the cup was nearly empty. He'd taken up too much of her time and could at least leave without leaving her his garbage. "No, I got it," he said. "I should let you get back to your little project."

"Okay." Her smile seemed a bit forced though. "Have a nice day."

She turned to go back to work as he turned towards the door wondering how he'd put his foot in his mouth that time. The woman with the unnaturally yellow hair was watching him leave. He raised a hand to wave to her and pushed the door open with the other hand, the one still holding the styrofoam cup. His hand slipped and splashed a few drips on the fancy wooden door. He groaned inwardly and tried to wipe it off with his fingers. That only smeared it. He got back on the sidewalk sure of one thing. He needed to buy his grandmother a new coffee maker.

3

The dog was on the table.

Trevor didn't know who had played it. If he asked, someone would give him a hard time about not paying attention. And he would deserve it. His head was not in the game.

He looked at Logan, who was his partner. Logan's eyes dropped to the dog and came back up with more than a little impatience. It was definitely his turn. Trevor looked at his hand as though he was merely having trouble deciding what to play. His hand was awful. There wasn't anything to think about. He tossed a pair of twos onto the table and tried to pay attention until everyone else was out.

Logan began to shuffle the cards. "All right, Trevor. We're only down by four hundred points. If you start playing now, we still have a chance."

"Four hundred *twenty*," Ryan said.

"That was a bad hand," Trevor said. "There wasn't anything I could do about it."

"And the one before it, where you had three aces and didn't call Tichu?" Logan wore a disapproving expression.

A missed Tichu did cost a hundred points. Trevor tried to defend himself. "A bomb would have easily stopped my pair."

"And you would have had one left," Logan said. "That's very recoverable."

"Plus, I didn't know Cameron was going to lead a full house." Trevor could tell Logan spotted the flaw in that logic the same time he did. He only needed to call Tichu before he played, not anyone else. He was saved by Cameron's interruption.

"I think it's my deal." He held his hand out to Logan for the cards.

Logan stopped shuffling to look at the score. "You sure?"

Cameron shrugged. "Pretty sure."

Logan counted the rounds, then handed the cards over.

"Have you had any luck with the online dating thing lately?" Ryan asked. He was looking at Cameron.

Cameron kept his eyes on the cards he was dealing. "No comment."

"Sounds like a no," Logan said.

Trevor smiled. "No luck is better than bad luck."

"For Cameron maybe," Ryan said, "but I kind of enjoy hearing about the bad luck."

"Me, too," Logan said. "What was the name of the one who turned out to be nearly as old as your mom?"

"Still not commenting." Cameron kept his eyes on the cards. His tone got a bit of an edge to it.

"And how many texts did you get from that other one before you blocked her number?" Logan looked at Cameron calmly, as though he was asking about the weather.

Cameron glared back. They knew he wasn't really annoyed, just not in the mood to talk about it. "Time to play," he said as he picked up his cards.

Logan looked at Trevor over his own hand. "He's talking to you."

Trevor didn't comment either. His cards looked promising.

"Well, I'm not ashamed to admit I'm still hoping for Cameron to have some good luck," Ryan said. "With someone who has a sister."

They all smiled because the doorbell rang as he said it, and the door opened at the same time so they knew whom it was.

"Hello, everyone." Audra breezed into the room.

"Hi, Audra," Logan said.

Trevor narrowed his eyes at her. "I see you still haven't figured out how to work a doorbell."

"I pushed it, didn't I?"

"But you didn't wait for an answer."

"I was doing you a favor so you didn't have to get up," she said. "Plus, the door was unlocked."

"I left it open for these guys," Trevor said, sweeping his arm around the table. "Not you."

"They're all here, and it was still unlocked." Audra smiled sweetly. "You left it open for me."

"It's open for you to leave, too," Ryan said.

She went around the table and shoved his arm. Ryan was also her brother, and he also lived there. Barging into their place wasn't enough so she attempted to push him off his chair. He was nearly twice her size so they both knew it wouldn't be effective.

Ryan gave her a playful shove in return and held his cards against his chest with his other hand. "Get out of here, Audra. You're not allowed to look at my cards."

"Why not?" she said. "I won't say anything."

He just shook his head without moving his cards.

She gave up with an exaggerated sigh and stepped aside to look over Logan's shoulder. He didn't try to hide his cards. Then she picked up his phone without asking to check the score. "Hmm." Audra frowned, then raised her eyebrows at Trevor. "Cards aren't cooperating tonight?"

He grunted in response, waiting for Logan to suggest it wasn't the cards.

Logan didn't contradict her. Audra had her hands pressed against the corner of the table near where she'd set down the phone.

He seemed to be staring at her hands. Trevor only noticed that because he was waiting for Logan to take his turn, and he didn't seem aware that it was his turn. Now who was distracted?

"Do you think he should pass?" Cameron asked.

He was looking at Audra, who raised her hands to deflect the question. She knew at least one of her brothers would yell at her if she made any comment about the contents of anyone's hand. Cameron knew that, too. He hadn't expected an answer and was only trying to alert Logan to the fact that it was his turn. Audra's movement seemed to get his attention.

"Oh, yeah," he said. "Pass."

Ryan collected his trick and tossed a low full house on the table. Audra flashed a quick smile before she squelched it. She schooled her features fine when she was playing but seemed to think no one noticed her reactions if she was only watching.

Trevor rolled his eyes to himself and tried to consider his hand as though he didn't know his partner had something that could beat it. He'd have to use a pair of kings to make a full house. He hated to waste them. But did it feel like a waste only because he knew he didn't need to use them? "Pass," he said.

Logan quickly went out and the round ended with their team getting a majority of the points, though of course they were still considerably behind. The next round had barely started when Audra tried to drift back behind Ryan. He held his cards out of her sight.

"Come on," she said. "I'm not going to say anything."

"Yeah, I know you won't *say* anything."

"What does that mean?" she asked.

"It means your poker face isn't as good as you think it is," Trevor said.

"Hey!" Logan turned on her. "Are you giving away my cards again?"

"I don't... think so." Audra set her face in defiance, but the uncertainty in her voice ruined the effect.

There were a few smiles. It was still a friendly game, after all. Logan held his cards closer to his chest but wasn't hiding them very effectively. Trevor kept his eyes away from his sister to avoid unwanted hints. He glanced up when Logan collected the cards to begin shuffling. Audra was giving him a strange look.

"Let's see what kind of poker face Trevor has if I mention that I talked to Grandma this afternoon," she said.

He knew his expression gave nothing away because he honestly didn't know why she seemed to think that would get a rise out of him.

Audra grinned wickedly. "She said you met someone."

Oh, dear. His brain scrambled to recall what he might have let slip before he was fully lucid.

Ryan raised an eyebrow. "A female someone?"

"That's what I hear," Audra said. She displayed a satisfied smirk.

Trevor shook his head at her. There was nothing to smirk about.

Logan saw the head shaking and put down the cards to turn to Audra. "What else do you hear?"

"Apparently Grandma sent Trevor to the place next door to get his coffee on Monday, and that's where this meeting occurred."

"Hang on." Ryan was figuratively scratching his head. "There's a hair salon on one side and some kind of furniture store on the other. Which of those places sells coffee?"

"Neither," Trevor said.

"The furniture place," Audra said at the same time.

The other guys should have been looking between them to see who would explain, but they were only looking at Audra.

"They don't sell coffee," Trevor said, cringing at what Alison must think of him taking it anyway.

"Grandma said there's a young woman who works there, and Trevor went over and sweet talked her into sharing."

He muttered, "That is definitely not what happened."

"What did happen?" Ryan asked.

Trevor motioned for Logan to start dealing. "Wait. Whose deal is it?"

Logan didn't hand the deck to anyone or even check to see who should get it. "I think you need to tell us about this sweet talking."

He could picture Alison's long hair swinging on her back as she walked. He tried to imagine what it might be like if he said something that made her turn around smiling because she was actually happy to see him and not because being friendly was part of her job. That was something he would likely never see.

Instead, he saw his sister looking very satisfied to catch him staring into space. "They don't sell coffee," Trevor repeated. "Grandma sent me over there groggy with no explanation, and I found this really pretty girl who gave me a cup. But it was a furniture store. She was sanding a table and there were no tables – I mean, for sitting at – and I didn't even know where she got the coffee. The situation was strange enough that I left without realizing I hadn't asked her how much I owed her for it." Trevor motioned to the cards again. It was time to get back to the game.

"You stole her coffee?" Logan said.

"The first time," Audra supplied helpfully.

Ryan looked way too interested. "Was there a second time?"

It didn't sound as though they were getting back to the game. "Yes, there was a second time," Trevor admitted. "Grandma was out of coffee again on Tuesday which, in hindsight, seems a little coincidental, but anyway... she suggested I head back, and I thought I should at least pay for it and... Alison told me it was complimentary... for *customers*. We both knew I wasn't a customer, and I brazenly asked for some anyway."

"Brazenly?" Logan said with a laugh.

"That's a Grandma word." Audra sounded just as amused. "What was so brazen about asking for coffee?"

"It was clearly the only reason I was there."

"Unless…" Audra grinned as all the guys turned to look up at her.

Ryan was the first to ask, "Unless what?"

"Unless she knew it *wasn't* the only reason."

It hadn't been. Trevor had jumped at the chance to pay for the coffee because he'd wanted to see her again. It had been too early for him to realize it was too early for him to make anything but a second disastrous impression. "She wasn't thinking that," he said.

"She might have been," Audra said. "She might have been flattered that you made an excuse to come back and see her. And maybe she's making extra coffee every day just in case you come back again."

Trevor shook his head at his sadly deluded sister. "No. Women are only flattered by guys making excuses to see them when it's a guy they want to see. There has never been a worse… I insulted her and her coworkers. I spilled coffee all over the place and just generally acted like an idiot. Both times. No one is hoping I go back." Except that he was. He couldn't concentrate on the game because he kept imagining scenarios where he talked to Alison and did not make a fool of himself.

"You don't know that for sure," Audra said. She was kind of hopeless.

"Did you really spill coffee twice?" Cameron asked.

"Well, not… yes." Trevor resigned himself to giving the gory details so they would all understand this was a lost cause. "The first time was worse. I tried to hand her my empty cup except it wasn't completely empty, and I am incapable of that simple task. I dropped the cup and drips got on her work. She had to use her shirt to clean it up. And the next day I fumbled the half-empty cup against the door when I was leaving. I don't think Alison saw that, but her coworker did. And I'm sure she told her."

"Is that the woman you said was creepy?" Audra asked.

Trevor glared at her. "How long did you talk to Grandma?"

"Long enough." She gave him a gloating smile. "How many different ways did you insult her?"

"Hang on. She was creepy?" Cameron looked as confused as he sounded. He had dark curly hair that he shoved off his forehead as though it was in the way of understanding. "Why are you interested in someone creepy?"

"I'm not."

"I think that was another woman," Logan said.

Audra laughed. "This is what happens when you make us extract information bits at a time," she said. "You need to just tell us all about her."

Trevor was sure he was already doing that. He certainly hadn't planned on sharing as much as he had. But his sister was far from satisfied.

"Or I could keep telling everyone Grandma's version," she said. "According to her, Trevor went over for coffee Monday and Tuesday, and he's been gushing about Alison the rest of the week. He thinks she has pretty hair."

"So Alison is not the name of the creepy woman?" Logan was looking to Audra for details now.

"No one was creepy," Trevor said. "There were two women working. One was Alison. She was young and pretty with long… And there was also an older woman, not old old but probably around Mom's age. She was kind of watching me some, but I'm sure paying attention to customers – or guys who wander off the street to bum coffee – is part of the job. She really wasn't being creepy, but I was cranky because it was early so I called her creepy and Alison kind of laughed so I went with it even though… She apparently changed her hair color between the times I was there and I think I said it looked weird or something but I was just... I was trying to figure out if it was the same woman."

"So you didn't actually insult Alison at all," Ryan said. "If she's not a fan of that coworker, you may not have messed up as bad as you think."

"Oh, no. I did." Trevor snatched the cards from in front of Logan – who had been absently shuffling them most of the time – and began to deal. He didn't care if it was his turn or not. After he explained how he had zero chance with Alison, they were going to talk about nothing but Tichu. "I called the stuff they were selling junk. I said I'd let her get back to her *little* project and I meant it literally because it was one of the smallest things there but I could tell she thought I was being dismissive and even when I tried to compliment her on a skill she was like, 'You're impressed that I can use a screwdriver?' Not to mention the fact that I interrupted her both times and generally acted like an idiot. I mean, I pointed to some jewelry they apparently sell for someone else and asked what it was. The stuff I'd just identified." He gave one last eye roll as he picked up his cards.

"What about –"

"No." Trevor cut off his sister. "We're done with that topic now."

"But what did you mean when you said they were selling the jewelry for someone else?" Audra asked.

"Oh. It sounded like she knows someone who makes jewelry. There was a display of mostly beaded things that really stuck out next to all the old furniture."

"And they sell it for her?"

Trevor looked up at the oddly eager tone in Audra's voice. Did she need more jewelry? She wore a necklace with a cross every day and must already have fifty of them.

"Are you thinking of your paintings?" Logan asked.

Audra nodded. "Did she tell you if they charge for floor space?"

"I really didn't get any details," he said.

The light in her eyes dimmed. "It's probably too much. And they probably only agreed to show the jewelry for someone they already knew."

"It wouldn't hurt to ask," Logan said. "Your work is good. And paintings make more sense than jewelry."

"Paintings make sense?" Trevor shot Audra a teasing glance before he moved his eyes to the painting behind her. It was one of hers, tall trees with shadows on a snowy background. She'd intentionally painted the snow on the undersides of the branches. Trevor honestly liked it, would have liked it even if he didn't know the artist, but he still gave her a hard time about it being backwards.

"I mean, to display next to furniture," Logan said. "They're both for the house."

"Your work *is* good," Ryan said. Perhaps because he was the oldest, he felt less need for a pretense of enmity between siblings. "I bet you could sell some."

"You could sell one right now," Logan said pointedly.

Audra gave his shoulder a shove. "Not funny."

"Not kidding," he said.

Trevor tapped the table next to Logan's cards. It really was past time to return to their game. Logan and Audra had an ongoing thing where he kept offering to buy a painting and she kept refusing and getting tense about it, too. She'd given one to everyone else she knew. In some cases, more than one. There was some reason Logan wasn't allowed to have one. If it was something other than both of them being stubborn, Trevor didn't want to know about it.

*A*lison was looking out the big front window thinking about what she might accomplish. She was wearing her professional clothes, including a skirt, because she had to go to an auction soon. She couldn't work on anything that involved sitting on the floor or messy liquids, which didn't leave her much that she wanted to do.

Of course, she didn't want to go to the auction either. But if she was going to take over the business one day, she needed to be able to do the tasks she didn't like. Alison smiled at a customer leaving as she sensed someone walking up to her other side.

The familiar white coffee mug was the first thing in her peripheral vision. "He'll be back."

Alison groaned inwardly at being so obvious. She was tempted to deny her reason for staring out the window. She settled on downplaying it. "Probably not," she said, "but it doesn't matter."

"I'm sure he will be." She lifted one hand from the mug – it was empty – to wave towards the sky. "The Holy Spirit brought him in here, and I could tell by the way he was looking at you that he'll be back."

"He was only here for coffee," Alison said.

"He *thought* he was here for coffee, but his guardian angel was whispering in his ear that something – someone – here was really good for him."

"Mom, you sound a little nuts."

Her mom cocked her head in a way that said Alison would be getting a lecture if she was still a child and not twenty-seven years old. "Why do I sound nuts? Angels are real."

"I know. But they're… they help protect us from physical and spiritual harm. They aren't matchmakers."

"Why not?" Her mom smiled but didn't back down. "Marriage is a sacrament of service. It's a man and a woman trying to bring out the best in each other, to help each other get to heaven. If God intends for a man to be married, why wouldn't his guardian angel nudge him towards someone who would make a good wife?"

Alison wasn't immediately sure how to answer. Marriage and angels were both created by God. It might have been theologically sound to suggest they worked together. But she still thought that trying to argue that was how she knew some random guy who wandered in for coffee was going to eventually marry her daughter was more than a little nuts.

"Plus…" Her mom waved a hand to indicate their surroundings. Then she nodded knowingly.

Alison snorted. "The shop isn't magic, Mom."

"I have never said magic," she said. "It's blessed."

"No, it's not." Alison tried not to roll her eyes at this familiar conversation, but she felt she wasn't entirely successful. "The shop was involved only because we spend a lot of time here. There's nothing divine in loosely related coincidences."

"Where is your faith, child? Don't put limits on what God can do."

"I'm not doubting God," Alison said. "I'm doubting *you*."

Her mom chuckled softly. "He's the one. You'll see." She started to lift her cup before she remembered it was empty and stopped.

Alison sent her eyes out the window briefly rather than to the ceiling. "You wouldn't be so sure if you were the one who talked to him. He insulted you, you know."

"Really? What did he say?" There was no offense in her tone, only curiosity.

"Never mind," Alison said. She hadn't meant to share that detail.

"Come on," her mom prompted. "I'm sure it wasn't that bad. He seemed like a nice young man."

"If you really want to know, he said you were creepy."

Her face was blank for a moment as she tipped her head to consider, then she said, "That's probably fair."

Alison laughed. "What do you mean that's fair?"

"Well, I was watching him pretty closely, trying to see his reaction to you and all. That might have come off a little creepy."

Alison had thought the same thing at the time. She'd known what her mom was up to and hadn't judged the guy too harshly for his comment. Now she was kind of annoyed to find out her mom had been aware of acting creepy. That was why she revealed something else she hadn't planned to share. "He also said your hair looked weird."

"Oh, it's awful." She ran a hand over her hair as she spoke. "Only two more days until I get it fixed. I really should have let her talk me out of it, but I thought the lighter shade would blend with the gray better. The tone is so wrong though."

"That doesn't make it okay for some stranger to point it out." Though she felt herself forgiving him in her head. He had seemed genuinely confused as to whether or not he was looking at the same woman and tripped over the words.

"I don't think he really meant to be insulting." Her mom flashed a smug smile. "If he had, you wouldn't be watching for him to come back." She turned to walk away as she added, "I need a refill."

Alison sighed before she realized she was in fact looking out the window again. What was it about that guy? She didn't even know his name and had to think of him as that guy, the one who stumbled in looking for coffee. She couldn't stop thinking about him, but it wasn't like a teenage crush. There was no fluttery feeling or breathless anticipation that he might return. It was more like a puzzle that was nagging at her. Everything about him prompted questions.

What was his name and why did he seem vaguely familiar? The feeling that someone was familiar was not at all uncommon in a small town. Most of the people Alison bumped into were people she'd seen before. She might have passed them walking their dogs, standing in line at the grocery store or at various town events. Why did it bug her so much that she couldn't place that guy? He seemed close enough in age that they might have been in school together, not in the same class because she was sure she'd remember that. But if he was a year or two older or younger, they might have passed each other in the hallways regularly.

She'd been out of high school for nine years though, and it would have been longer if he was older. Surely that was too much time for an impression to stick. Unless they'd had some interaction. Her name hadn't meant anything to him though. Surely if they'd had a class together or a club or something, he'd have asked if she was Alison Brachy from such and such. She didn't want to think she was the more forgettable one.

Alison had noticed his smile, with one tooth on the bottom more forward than the rest for some character. She'd noticed his eyes, too, pale blue and nicely shaped. But there was something behind them that grabbed her attention, something that begged her to see a nice guy in spite of the clumsy words.

Maybe the guy who came in for coffee wasn't actually familiar to her. Maybe she'd only tricked herself into thinking that as an excuse to keep bringing him to mind. Maybe because she recognized him the second day, she convinced herself that she remembered him from something earlier as well. That would have made her reaction more reasonable. She'd been way too excited to see the guy who'd been kind of a jerk the previous day.

He'd barely thanked her. He'd insulted her furniture as well as her mother. Alison felt a little guilty that the barbs at her projects stung more, but her mom had admitted she deserved it. The wooden pieces had done nothing to him.

She and her parents didn't just pick up any old junk though, they only added junk they knew they could make beautiful again. His failure to recognize the difference should have been a huge turnoff. Instead, she found herself wondering why it wasn't. His demeanor had been so much more bumbling than arrogant. Was there something in his life he was struggling through? Was it something that could make her interest more sympathetic than romantic? Not that she'd diagnosed it as romantic. She was only curious.

A customer came in to distract her for a while, but she was curious enough that she found herself checking the sidewalk through the front window a couple more times that morning. It wasn't until she went to the auction that she pushed all thoughts of the coffee guy from her head.

She had to be professional as she handed out business cards. She had to focus and smile as she told people that if they needed any help fixing up the old furniture they bought, she knew just the place. She had to be friendly and confident when she told others that if they didn't find what they were looking for, they might find it at Next Love.

Two hours of hobnobbing, as her dad called it, was way more exhausting than two hours of pounding nails and turning screws. Alison had bought one piece herself. They didn't need more inventory at the moment, but she couldn't resist the chair with the intricately carved pattern on the back. It had been practically free because the wood had warped to make the legs wobble. She could fix that. She could make it the perfect addition to someone's furniture collection.

It was well past lunch by the time she got it into the back of her truck. Her stomach was grumbling rather angrily. She slammed the tailgate. The bang was a satisfying punctuation to her being finished with the chore. She stopped at a fast-food place on her way back to the shop and sat in a corner by herself, happy to have a few minutes with her own company.

She reflected that her parents had a nice arrangement. Her dad generally hid in the back of the shop working on the furniture while her mom actually enjoyed chatting with customers. Alison was somewhere in the middle. She worked in the shop where she could talk to the customers, but she preferred they stay on the subject of furniture and not delve into local news or invite personal questions as her mom often did. It was a dream to have a partner to help run the shop when she took over, and her mind unwittingly went to that guy who wanted coffee. She doubted he had the social skills to let her hide in the back with her dad.

Her phone buzzed. And it was her dad. She smiled at the interesting timing as she answered. "Hi, Dad. I was just thinking about you."

"About how I'm the best dad ever?"

She laughed. "Something like that."

"I'm glad to hear you're in a good mood," he said, "because I'm calling to ask a favor."

"Oh, boy."

"A young woman came in just after you left. Your mom talked to her. Apparently, she wants to know if there's any chance we'd be willing to sell some of her art in the shop."

"What kind of art?" Alison asked.

"Painting, I gather."

"Hmm. What do you and Mom think about that?"

"Your mom loves the idea. She said paintings on the wall would make the place more homey and encourage people to envision our pieces in their own homes." He sounded amused.

Alison also thought it was sort of funny. She could picture her mom saying it, yet she couldn't picture paintings making the shop homey. The overall atmosphere was more warehouse than house, and decorations wouldn't change that. "Our walls *are* bare," she observed neutrally.

"I see you agree your mom is nuts," he said. "I think she's looking for a reason to make it in our interest to help the girl out."

"Did she really like her work then?"

"The young woman didn't bring any paintings with her."

"Did she at least have pictures?" Alison asked. "It would be awfully embarrassing to agree to display her work and then find out it looks like something Annabelle did at preschool." Annabelle was her 4-year-old niece.

"It would," her dad said, suddenly speaking slowly, "and this is where the favor comes in."

Alison said nothing. She was afraid her parents had already decided the work was no good and wanted her to be the one to break the news. But she remembered the woman hadn't brought anything to judge.

"Your mom made an appointment for someone to view the paintings at 2 o'clock," he continued. "I can go if you're not back, but I'm hoping you're going to be back. You're not still at the auction, are you?"

"No, I stopped for lunch. I'm right around the corner."

"Great!" He sounded relieved. "She lives here in town. Do you want her name and address so you can go straight there?"

Alison checked her watch. She'd have to stall over her nearly finished lunch for a while. "No. I have time to drop off the chair I bought. I'll be there in a few minutes, and you can give me all the details then."

"Okay. Hurry back."

She stuffed a few fries in her mouth as she put the phone away, suddenly feeling in a hurry. She cleared away her trash and headed out to her truck. Her dad was waiting by the back door of the shop to help her unload.

He climbed onto the truck bed and ran a hand over the chair back. "Very nice," he said. "I knew you weren't planning to buy anything so when you said you did, I expected something special. Very nice." He continued to examine the chair as Alison untied it. "The seat is too thin," he said. "We'll need to reinforce it, I think."

"I was thinking of adding a cushion."

He nodded thoughtfully. "A little comfort would improve functionality, and we," he smiled, "*you* would have an easier time hiding the patching with fabric."

That was exactly Alison's reasoning. She knew it was good, but she still liked to hear the approval in her dad's voice. She hopped off the back of the truck, and he handed the chair down to her.

"What do we know about these paintings?" she asked.

He groaned.

It had nothing to do with her question. At sixty-two, he could no longer hop off the back and had to climb. He seemed pretty spry despite the sound effects. Alison wondered if – and hoped – it might be exaggerated, perhaps more like a kihap than an expression of actual pain.

He moved ahead to open the door for her once he was on the ground, then faced her as he held it open. "Well, like I said, your mom talked to her. She's already excited, talking about how it'll brighten the whole place and make people linger and… something about a marriage of ideas."

Alison fit the chair inside and set it against a wall for later. They had a garage-style door for larger pieces. "So what you're saying," she said, "is that if I don't like this art, I'm going to disappoint the artist *and* Mom."

He shrugged and reached into his back pocket. He pulled out a notecard folded in half and wrinkled. "Here's the girl's info."

Alison unfolded the card to find a name, address and phone number in her mom's very neat handwriting. Then she checked her watch. "I suppose I should head over there."

"Just find out if the work would make a good impression on our customers," he said, "and tell her we'll get back to her. We'll talk and work out details before we agree to anything."

Alison nodded and stepped outside with the card still in her hand. She knew the town well and recognized the street name. Given that there was a letter after the address, she guessed it was the big house. Older people in town called it the Founder's Mansion. It was a huge house built in the late 1800s. That was something like fifty years after the town was founded so Alison didn't know how the name became attached.

She was happy to see that the address out front matched the one on her instructions as she parked in front of it. She'd never been inside the cool house. It was huge by house standards but perhaps a little small for a real mansion. It had been converted many years ago, before Alison was born, into five small apartments. She got this number from the mailboxes lined up at the street.

While a lot of apartments were heavy on symmetry, keeping all the units the same, this one had two doors on the front, one farther to the left than the other was to the right, and a door on each side, in different places. Alison had never been able to determine from driving by where the fifth door was, though she assumed it was on the back. She was looking for unit A now, which was the front left.

She flipped down the visor to check her teeth for remnants of lunch, which would not convey a professional appearance. As she pushed it back up, she noticed someone had come out of the side apartment. And she recognized him. It was the guy who'd come in for coffee.

This was her chance to ask his name. Hopefully, that would trigger the memory that seemed to be just out of reach and get him out of her head. But as soon as he locked the door behind himself, he jogged across the lawn to a car, presumably his, and jumped inside.

Alison wasn't going to flag him down if he was in a hurry. She might not have been able to catch him anyway. She stayed in the truck until he drove away. Now she wondered why he was in a hurry. That wasn't going to help her forget about him.

5

*A*lison got out of the truck with a deep breath, preparing herself once again to be a qualified representative of Next Love. Her grandparents had named the shop, and she was so used to it she rarely gave any thought to whether or not it was a good name. But every now and then, someone would react in a way that questioned it. Or would question it outright. That guy who came in for coffee was the latest. She wasn't thinking about him though.

Audra Norman. That was the name on the card and her focus. There had been someone named Ryan Norman in Alison's class in high school. Given that they lived in a small town, the chance that they were related was pretty good. She tucked away that nugget for later. If she found herself standing awkwardly in front of ugly paintings, she could suddenly remember to ask Audra if she knew Ryan. That could put them on a safe subject before she made an exit.

Alison stepped up to the door. She pulled her hand back before touching the doorbell and gave a confident knock instead. She didn't feel confident, despite knowing she had all the power in the situation. She was going to do her best to act confident though.

The door was opened by a young woman with pale blonde hair. There was a crease in it, above her shoulders, that looked as though she'd just pulled out a rubber band. Her smile appeared genuinely confident. "Hello," she said. "Are you from the furniture store?"

"Yes." Alison held out a hand. "Alison Brachy."

"Alison?" The young woman repeated the name as though it meant something to her. Perhaps she was someone who remembered names by connecting them to someone or something she already knew.

Alison simply nodded.

"I'm Audra." She gave a quick handshake, then waved her arm for Alison to follow her inside.

They entered through a short hallway that opened into a living room covered with artwork. There were paintings sitting along the couch and propped on the floor in front of it. There were paintings along one wall. Strangely, it didn't appear that any of the art was actually hung on the wall but stacked three high against it with the bottommost at a slight angle at the carpet. Most of the canvases were the same size, but one twice the size of the others had been laid flat on the floor. The scene was an overwhelming quantity of shapes and colors for one room.

Audra began to spill words in a rush before Alison could process any of it. "I've gotten out as much as I could for you to look at. You see I have way too much of it. That's why it'd be awesome if I could find a way to get rid of some of it without just getting rid of it. You know what I mean, right? I'm not really looking to make a living off of this or anything. But it would be nice if I could get enough to pay for some supplies. It's kind of an expensive hobby. I don't know whether I'm more excited or terrified by the idea of putting my work out for others to see, but I've been trying not to think too much about either since I know it's a remote possibility anyway. I can hardly believe you even... well, I'll just give you a minute to look them over, and then you can tell me what you think."

Alison took that as permission to step closer. So far, she could see that they were landscapes. One had caught her eye as Audra neared the end of her speech. The shadows were wrong. It was a rather stark picture of birch trees in neat rows, but the shadows were going towards the sun and not away from it. It was wrong, and yet it didn't look wrong because it had clearly been painted that way on purpose.

Just below it, she found a painting of a mountain at sunset. There were all kinds of foothills in the foreground with different bushes and shrubs and hints of animals hiding in them. The detail was amazing, but Alison's eyes kept going back to the mountain until she realized why. It was too bright. The peak seemed to be the source of the light that the sky reflected rather than the other way around. How had Audra made it look so natural?

Alison moved quickly to study another painting. This one was a forest scene full of many shades of green with a little babbling brook running through the middle. Her eyes searched for something that didn't belong. There was a gentle rain shower in the picture that she hadn't noticed at first, but now she could see it in the tiny circles in the water and the way some of the leaves were turned up to catch the drops. The ripples in the stream were… Alison smiled as she caught the anomaly. The land was sloped the other way. It appeared that the water was flowing uphill.

She was about to take her attention to another picture when movement to her right reminded her that the artist was waiting for an opinion. She tore herself away to focus on Audra. "These are really good," she said.

Audra bit the side of her lip and widened her eyes as though she was waiting for more. She seemed to want to hear it again before she believed it.

"Seriously," Alison said. "I am very impressed."

"Thank you." Audra sort of lit up all over as her eyes sparkled and her heels bounced up and down. "I've gotten a lot of compliments but only from friends and family so it really means something that someone unbiased likes my work."

"I really do." Alison had let her vision drift back to another painting. It was a field of wildflowers, colorful yet subtle. There were tons of different shapes and colors of flowers, but they were all tiny.

The picture was still mostly green with a blue sky. She could imagine herself sitting on a hill watching a breeze make the flowers dance.

"What's wrong?" Audra asked.

Alison realized that she was frowning at the painting. "Nothing," she said quickly. "It's beautiful. I'm just... I can't find the anomaly in this one."

"Oh. There isn't one in that one." Audra smiled a bit self-consciously. "Not everyone appreciates my *kooky* landscapes. That's what my grandpa calls them. So I make some plain."

"Do you paint anything besides landscapes?"

"Not too much." She motioned to a painting across the room. "I've done a few through a window, like that one, where there's some interior on the edge. I'd love to do people, but whenever I try, the eyes come out sad. In every sense."

"In what sense? Senses?" Alison did not understand.

"Sad as in not very good," Audra said, "and also sad as in... sad. No matter what scene I'm imagining, the people on the canvas end up looking like they don't want to be there. It's weird. I can't figure out what I'm doing wrong."

Alison was entertained by the description but tried not to show it because Audra sounded frustrated behind her smile. Then worry replaced the smile.

"Is that a problem?" Audra asked. "Are landscapes not what you're looking for?"

"I don't know what we're looking for, but there's a chance this is it." Alison swept her eyes across the room of beautiful artwork. When they returned, Audra looked so excited she knew she needed to reign in her own enthusiasm. Alison wasn't supposed to commit to anything yet.

If word got out about these paintings on display, they'd probably see an increase in foot traffic, which would not hurt their business. Plus, she noticed that none of these paintings had been framed. That was something she could do for buyers. But any business deal should be carefully considered, and Alison was only there for fact-finding. "All right," she said, "let's talk about some practical things."

Audra nodded seriously. Her lips were pressed together against a smile that clearly wanted out.

"We'd need you to sign something that says we're not liable if anything happens to the paintings."

"Okay." Audra nodded without the least concern.

"I mean, we have insurance if there was like a fire or something, but if a careless customer knocked one off the wall or something that –"

"I'm not worried," Audra said. "Life happens." She didn't look worried.

Alison, on the other hand, was thinking of a particular careless customer who had spilled coffee on her work. She was worried about how unsuccessful she was at getting him out of her head. New question. "How much space do you think you'd want to display your work?"

"Whatever you'd… If they're clustered up, and you don't mind nails in the wall… half a dozen wouldn't take up much space. But I'd love more space if you can spare it."

Alison nodded now, trying to think of anything else she should ask. She thought of all the conversations regarding Sheila and her jewelry. She remembered that her dad had never been fully comfortable handling money for someone else and only agreed because she was a family friend. "We'd probably want you to handle your own transactions. That would involve maybe posting a phone number for customers to contact you or being in the shop personally at set times. Do you have thoughts on that?"

"I think I'd rather do that in person. I don't want to…" She crinkled her eyes in concentration. "Would Saturday work? Saturday mornings would work well with my schedule."

"I think so." Alison gave it some thought. "You could hang a whiteboard to let people know when you'll be in. It'd be easy to change if you wanted to try a different time."

"Oh, I could decorate it." Audra continued to look more and more thrilled.

Alison continued trying to be practical. She thought again of the jewelry they had on display and how she fielded almost as many questions about the woman who made it as the product itself. Some background information would be helpful if they agreed to display the paintings. "How long have you been painting?"

"Well, I've always loved drawing and different types of art. It wasn't until sometime in high school that I settled on oils as my favorite medium." Before Alison could ask how long ago that was, she added, "I know, I'm only twenty-two so most people would say that's not very much experience, but five or six years feels like a long time to me. Especially when I see how many I've accumulated in that time."

"How long does it take you to finish one?"

"Oh, it varies. Sometimes I'll spend weeks and weeks just thinking about an idea so that by the time I get out the brushes, I can create it in only a few hours. Sometimes I keep scraping off paint and restarting and... I don't know. By the time I'm done I don't even remember what I first started to paint."

"Is this everything you've painted?" Alison swept her arm around the room. She meant that she was impressed Audra kept it all, but realized she might sound dismissive, as though there wasn't enough to sell. "I mean, where do you keep it when it isn't spread around the room?"

"In the closet," Audra said. "My roommate gives me a hard time because I got all the paintings unpacked and tucked into the closet, but my clothes are still in boxes in the bedroom."

"Have you not lived here very long?"

"Uh…" A guilty smile crept over her face. "It's been almost three years," she said, then laughed.

Alison laughed with her.

"I've always loved this old house," Audra continued. "I was really excited to find one of the apartments available. But I was kind of disappointed when I first saw it. I mean, the outside has the gables and turrets and cool old details and the inside is just… well, bland." She shrugged at her surroundings. "White walls, tan carpet, nothing that says you're living in a hundred-and-some-year-old house. But… it was still what we were looking for in terms of size and price, and there aren't a ton of apartments in town."

Alison only nodded. She still lived with her parents and was in the habit of keeping quiet when others talked about finding or choosing a place to live. She wasn't embarrassed by her situation, only aware that she had no experience to add to the conversation.

"It's a good place though," Audra said, "and the landlord is nice. I even convinced him to let my brother take one of the other apartments a few months after I moved in."

"Your brother?" Alison said. She was about to ask if that was Ryan Norman, whom she knew from school.

But Audra spoke again first. "Yes. He's kind of obsessed with you. I hope you'll give him a chance if –" She slapped a hand over her mouth so fast she seemed to startle herself. "I can't believe I said that. Pretend I didn't. He'd be so mad if he knew I was talking about him, and for good reason. We're talking about my work *only*." She turned towards the paintings to illustrate the direction of the discussion. "What else do you need to know?"

There were a few things Alison wanted to know. She saw Ryan at church occasionally. He was in the choir. If they happened to pass each other coming in or going out, there would be nods and greetings and a general acknowledgment that they were familiar to each other. There hadn't been anything that would count as a conversation in ten years. While it was beyond flattering to imagine he'd been secretly obsessed with her for that long, it was also incredibly unlikely. Now she'd be wondering the next time she bumped into him, which might be weird.

Alison couldn't very well pump the woman she barely knew for information though. Even if Audra didn't look distressed by her slip, it wouldn't be right to talk about someone who wouldn't appreciate being their subject.

The paintings were an impressive redirect. Once Alison stepped closer again, it was easy to give them her full attention. "What made you want to do... did you call them *kooky* landscapes?"

"My grandpa's word," Audra said with a fond smile. "He insults my work, but he's hung one in nearly every room in their house. I don't really remember a specific decision to make the kooky ones my thing, and I know I'm not the first person to paint that way. I just remember that I made some happy accidents when I was still learning about angles and shadows and things. At some point, I started doing it on purpose."

"So you did take some classes?"

"Yeah. A few in high school. A few more in college."

Alison nodded. She was paying attention even though her eyes were engrossed in the ripples of a pond.

"I didn't finish so I don't have a degree in art."

"How do you decide what to... what you want to change?"

"There's some trial and error in that," Audra admitted. "Some of them have been awful. One time, I tried to reverse the color of some trees. It was an autumn scene. I painted the trunks in reds and yellows and a bit of purple, and I did the leaves in shades of brown. I could tell it wasn't working pretty early, but I kept going anyway because... I don't know. It was like someone vomited on the canvas. In the end, it was a terrible waste of paint."

Alison was intrigued. Based on what was in front of her, it was difficult to picture Audra capable of wasting paint. "How do you know when it *is* working?"

"Huh." Audra froze as though the question surprised her. Then she broke into a happy smile with a shrug.

Alison didn't resist the urge to reflect the smile. Already in the very short acquaintance, Audra gave the impression of having a sunshiny personality. It wasn't just her hair, though the yellowy color might have helped. That guy who asked for coffee had dark blond hair. Had his been bright like that when he was a boy? And why was Alison asking herself that question when Audra was addressing a more interesting one?

"My grandma says that my paintings make people take a closer look at God's creation, that they make people think about why he made things the way he did and how chaotic things would be if we didn't have such an intelligent designer. And I'm always too busy saying, 'Grandma, I'm not that deep,' to pay much attention to what I'm actually thinking. I just know the kookiness shouldn't be the first thing that catches the eye."

"That makes sense," Alison said. She could study the paintings for some time, which made her realize how long she'd already been looking at them. "I think I've taken up enough of your time. I'll need to discuss it with management so it'll be a couple of days until we're in touch about whether or not we can work together."

Alison felt a twinge of nostalgia as she spoke. She and her sisters had started referring to their parents as management when the oldest, Angela, had started working in the shop. Their parents were in charge so it was an appropriate word, and yet the sisters always laughed when it was used. Alison sometimes missed working with her sisters.

"Okay," Audra said. She was barely containing her excitement, hopefully at the possibility and not because of anything she thought was already arranged.

"Can I take a few pictures to show management?" Alison asked. "I won't show anyone else."

Audra gave a quick nod.

After a few snaps with the phone, Audra walked her to the door while she made sure Alison had the correct phone number to contact her with a decision. "And you're really going to forget I said anything about my brother, right?"

"Right." Alison said it as a reflex because she had almost forgotten about it. Until of course Audra brought it up again. She didn't roll her eyes at that. She only wished her a nice day.

Then Alison thought about it as she walked back to her truck. It couldn't really mean what it sounded like, but what if it did? What if she acted stiff and awkward the next time she ran into Ryan? Would things stay weird, or should Alison perhaps try to think about Ryan more while she tried to think of coffee guy less?

*R*yan spread an impressive straight on the table. "Now as long as no one has a bomb," he said.

"Bomb!" Logan put four kings on top of the straight.

"Are you kidding me?" Trevor gaped at him. "That's like your third one tonight?"

Logan held up four fingers.

Trevor shook his head in disbelief as Ryan groaned.

Cameron smiled. He was on Logan's team and enjoying their good luck.

A minute later, Ryan tossed his unplayed cards onto the table. "Well, the good news is they beat us fast enough that we have time for another game."

Logan checked the score. "1085 to 215. With four double go-outs. That *was* really fast."

"We don't need the recap," Ryan said.

"Okay. Let's see who has to move." Logan switched to a different app and set his phone in the middle of the table. Each guy put a finger on the screen for it to randomly assign teams.

Trevor changed seats to be across from Logan. Now that they were on the same team, he didn't expect to see any more bombs coming from Logan's hand. He was already shuffling the cards. Trevor absently ran his finger back and forth over a scratch on the table. There were more on this side.

"Are you going to pick up your cards or continue to meditate on the scratch pattern?" Logan asked. There was clear amusement in his voice.

Trevor looked up to see that the other three already had their cards sorted and ready to pass. He was still thinking about the table. Though not really. His mind was really on the woman who made him notice the scratches on the table. He picked up his cards.

There was a fifty-fifty split on the points that hand and nothing interesting enough to draw his attention from Alison. Maybe he should ask the guys if they thought his plan was bold or stupid. Or both. Logan was shuffling, and Trevor didn't know whose turn it was to deal. He might as well admit he was distracted. "Is it my deal?"

Logan nodded. He made no move to hand over the cards.

"I've decided to try to talk to Alison again."

"The one you threw coffee at?" Ryan asked.

"I didn't throw coffee at *her*."

"Sounded like you kind of did."

He'd passed a cup too quickly and let go too quickly and coffee sprayed out and ended up on her shirt. Maybe he had kind of thrown coffee at her. "I'm going to look for her tomorrow afternoon, when I'm fully awake. I mean, I don't even know if she works on Saturdays so I don't know if it'll work."

"You're just going to walk in there and ask for her without any kind of pretense?" Ryan sounded impressed.

Because he was wrong.

"Well, no." Trevor ran his finger over another mark in the wood. "I'm going to ask her about this table."

Logan laughed. "You're gonna tell her you think about her whenever you look at your crappy old table?"

The others laughed while Trevor made a mental note to be careful with his wording. What Logan said was completely true, but phrasing it that way in front of Alison would not help him out of the hole he'd dug on previous encounters. "I thought that since they buy old furniture and fix it up when they resell it, maybe they could fix up some old furniture I already own."

"That does sound like a reasonable question," Cameron said.

Trevor opened his mouth to thank him for the support.

Before he could, Cameron turned to Ryan and Logan and said, "I bet he couldn't think of anything to buy from her."

His mind had gone there first. There was no denying it so Trevor only glared at his friends for being entertained by it.

"The table is pretty beat up," Ryan conceded. "But it hasn't bothered you before."

"It doesn't bother me now," Trevor said. "I just thought... it'll probably last longer with a little care. It'll be an investment."

"You don't sound very convincing." Logan finally quit shuffling and set the cards in front of Trevor. "She's going to see right through you."

"You think?" Trevor began to deal slowly.

"Undoubtedly," Logan said.

Cameron was nodding.

Ryan was as well, but he seemed thoughtful. "That might not be a bad thing though," he said. "If she knows you're interested, she might be able to give you some hints on whether or not she minds while you still have the pretense up. Better than an obvious crash and burn."

"Good point," Logan said.

"That's assuming I notice and correctly interpret said hints."

"Better point," Logan said.

Trevor laughed with the rest. There was no barb in agreeing he might miss something, not when it came from a group of guys who had also had poor luck with women.

Cameron had eventually signed up for the matching site after he found out thirdhand that his girlfriend was dating someone else. Ryan had had at least four women tell him they'd rather stay friends.

One of them called him not even a week later to ask for advice about a guy she was interested in. And she said that. She'd said, "There's this guy I *am* interested in." Logan had never made much effort to not be single. Trevor had some suspicions about that.

He heard his doorbell as the object of those suspicions waltzed into his apartment. "Good evening, gentlemen," Audra said.

"Why do you sound sarcastic?" Ryan said. "You are addressing gentlemen."

She just rolled her eyes at him. "How's the game going?"

"It's over," Logan said.

"Then why are you holding cards?"

He grinned in response.

"Oh, so you won a quick one," Audra guessed. "Who was on your team?"

"I'll give you one hint. It wasn't either of your brothers."

She smiled congratulations at Cameron, then said, "They would not have been my first guesses anyway."

"Thanks." Ryan threw out some sarcasm of his own. "This game won't be nearly as short if Logan doesn't pass some cards."

"Oh, right." He sounded as though he'd forgotten that part of the game before he began to study his cards.

Audra moved behind him to look over his shoulder. Her lips pinched against a smile.

"Audra." Trevor said her name as a warning.

"My poker face is fine," she said.

He shook his head.

She sighed as she took a step back and to the side. She could still see Logan's cards from there but was no longer directly in Trevor's line of sight. He could more easily avoid accidental hints. He did notice her checking her phone while they finished the hand.

"You still haven't heard?" Trevor asked.

She shook her head, looking frustrated.

Logan glanced back curiously. "You're waiting on a phone call?"

"Of course," she said. "You guys didn't tell him about my meeting?"

"Sorry, sis." Trevor didn't sound sorry because he wasn't. "We don't exactly get together to discuss you."

Audra wrinkled her nose in disgust. "But this is big. Or it could be." She focused on Logan with glances at Cameron. "I contacted the people at Next Love, that furniture store Trevor was talking about last week where they have someone's jewelry for sale. She seemed to really like my work. And she said they would let me know in a few days. It's already been a few days."

"That does sound exciting," Logan said. "But maybe you should reign it in until you know for sure."

"You don't think they'll work with me?"

"I... you just said you don't know yet."

"But I think they will. She really liked my pictures and..." Audra's eyes sparkled with enthusiasm. "I already bought a whiteboard I can put on my old easel to say when I'll be in. She said I'd probably have to be available to handle sales in person. Sales! That means people buying my paintings. Wouldn't that be so cool? But it won't be a lot of money so I'll just report it as hobby income to keep things... what?"

Logan was wincing. "You worry me with all these plans. It sounds like you're setting yourself up for devastation if they turn you down."

Her arms quickly folded across her chest. "Why would they turn me down? Because my paintings aren't good enough?"

"No." Logan was holding the cards. He began to shuffle with a deliberate calm. "I'm sure if they don't agree to display your work, it'll be some other... like maybe a space issue or something."

"She did say she had to discuss practical things with management."

"I wonder if the creepy lady is the boss," Trevor said, mostly to himself.

"Plus…" Audra was suddenly fighting a smile. "I doubt I'll be *devastated* to not have to calculate hobby income on my taxes."

"That's not what I meant," Logan said.

Ryan laughed. "Taxes aside, Logan does sort of have a point about you being a little cart before the horse, as Grandma May would say."

"Whose deal is it?" Logan held up the cards.

Trevor nodded to Cameron, who took the deck and began to deal from it.

Audra was still releasing a sigh. "Guys, I know it might not happen. I can enjoy the idea without being crushed if it doesn't work out."

Trevor kept quiet about her not being the only one who enjoyed the idea. He was thinking that he could help her transport the artwork to the shop. Perhaps even on a regular basis.

"I do wish she'd hurry up and let me know though." Audra pulled her phone out just enough to flash the screen before she shoved it back into her pocket.

"I have a question." Logan had picked up a few cards. He set them face down on the table to turn to Audra. "You keep saying she. Have you been talking to Alison or the creepy lady or someone else from the store?"

"Alison. I found out her last name is Brachy." She glanced at Trevor as though this was a crucial piece of the puzzle.

"Alison Brachy?" Ryan's ears perked up. "I went to school with her."

"She was in your class?" Audra asked.

He nodded.

"So she's older than Trevor." Audra looked at him again, apparently gauging his reaction.

Trevor shrugged at her. That would make Alison no more than three years older than him. He would have guessed younger, but it didn't matter.

"She goes to Holy Trinity, too," Ryan said.

"Really?" There was something that mattered. "Why have I never seen her there?" Trevor asked.

"Because you go on Saturday."

Trevor considered this useful information. He could potentially start getting up early on Sundays to see her. If it wasn't a terrible idea.

Logan tapped the table near Ryan. "Point her out to me this weekend."

Ryan nodded.

Trevor wondered if the information was worth having everyone dissect his love life. Or current lack thereof.

"What did you think of Alison?" Logan asked Audra.

"She seemed really nice." Audra said this encouragingly, as though her brother might be looking for her approval.

He ignored her.

"Pretty, too," she added.

It was past time to get this round started. Trevor pulled a three out of his hand for Ryan. He had three aces so he could spare one of those for Logan.

"Why do you look guilty?" Logan asked.

"I don't look guilty," Audra said, very quickly. Too quickly.

"You sound guilty, too."

Trevor looked up to see his sister shaking her head at Logan.

"It's nothing," she said.

Were they still talking about Alison?

"Are we going to pass some cards or what?" Cameron said. He was clearly talking about Tichu.

That was a better conversation. Trevor nodded at him and shoved his cards towards their recipients.

"I hate to hold up the game," Logan said.

Ryan made a scoffing noise before he could finish the statement.

Logan tried to look shocked, but he couldn't pull it off. He knew as well as anyone that he was most often accused of holding up the game. "I really think we need to hear what Audra is hiding though. It obviously has to do with her talking to Alison so I think Trevor is in trouble."

"You sound real concerned for him," Ryan said.

Neither of them was doing much to hide their amusement. Even Cameron seemed in no hurry to play if delaying meant hearing about Trevor being in trouble. Trevor began to wonder if Audra had actually done something that should concern him.

"It's no big deal," she said.

And now he was concerned. "What did you do?"

Her eyes softened into a pleading expression. "Please don't be mad."

Trevor groaned. "Come on, Audra. Nothing good has ever come after the words, 'Please don't be mad.'"

"Well, I was talking with Alison when she came to look at my paintings, and we were talking about the paintings. I think. I don't remember exactly how it happened because I knew we weren't talking about you, but somehow I mentioned how you were obsessed with her before I realized the words were coming out of my mouth and I just changed the subject real fast so I don't think she paid it any attention, maybe didn't even catch what I said. It's fine. It's... fine."

It wasn't difficult to hear what Audra was trying to hide in her stream of words. The other guys at the table were snickering. "Did you actually use the word obsessed?" Trevor asked.

"Kind of."

"That is a yes or no question."

"I said you were *kind of* obsessed," Audra said. "And I was more talking to myself than her so I probably mumbled it. I bet she didn't hear it. She didn't react like she noticed. I mean, I didn't really watch for a reaction because I was trying to get everyone's attention back on the paintings. You're not mad, right?"

"No," he said. Being mad would be childish. It would also suggest he had something to hide. He wasn't obsessed with anyone. He'd accidentally mentioned Alison to his grandma a few times. He'd talked about her during the previous week's game only because someone else brought her up. It was true he'd spent a lot of time thinking about a reason he could return to her store. But not an unhealthy amount. And no one else knew how much time anyway. Trevor threw a jack onto the trick to finally continue the game. Finally.

"You let him win with a jack?" Cameron said as Trevor collected the cards.

Ryan shrugged. "So did you."

Unfortunately, it was one of the only tricks Trevor won that hand. He stared at his leftover cards and wondered if he could have played something differently.

"What are you going to say when you ask about the table?" Audra asked.

He could have played the aces one at a time, but he had the dragon and couldn't predict so many singleton tricks. It was a shame that a great hand had been so unlucky.

Audra rapped her knuckles on the table to get his attention.

Trevor tossed his cards in the center to be reshuffled and met her impatient eyes without answering.

"What are you going to say?" she repeated.

Audra hadn't arrived yet when he'd admitted his ruse to visit Alison. Logan had gone out first. Trevor was vaguely aware that they'd been talking afterwards, still about Alison. Perhaps Audra was the one obsessed.

"I'm going to ask if she'll fix up this old table."

"How?" she pressed.

Trevor wasn't interested in whatever role-playing Audra wanted. He pretended to misinterpret. "If I knew how to fix a table, I wouldn't have to ask," he said. "I'm just going to show her a picture and see if she can improve it."

"That's lame," Audra said.

"What is?" Trevor didn't really want her opinion. He expected a request for more details though and was caught off guard by the negative response.

"You can't just ask if she might be able to *improve* the table." Audra stressed the word improve as though it was offensive. "It'll be obvious you're making up an excuse to talk to her."

Logan smiled. "It's kind of late for you to be worried about him being obvious, isn't it?"

She shot him a glare that said he should stay out of it before she refocused on her brother. "I don't mean like... An excuse in this case might make her feel like you're wasting her time or that you won't appreciate her work." She leaned forward to brush her fingers across the surface with a thoughtful expression. "You need to ask her for something specific – maybe even something special – so she knows it's something you actually want."

Trevor reluctantly admitted, to himself, that Audra had a point. There was a difference between an excuse to talk to Alison and an excuse to put her to work. He'd convinced himself that he really wanted the table refinished. He only hadn't noticed how beat up it looked before. But if Alison wasn't convinced, she might feel patronized. Trevor didn't have to humble himself to ask his little sister for advice. She was more than willing to offer it unasked.

"I got it," she said. "When I was in there, I saw a table in the front with the finished pieces. See how you can make out the little lines in the wood... Do they call that the grain? Anyway, the other table had somehow emphasized those so it almost looked like a relief map. It was cool."

Trevor shook his head. He didn't want a relief map on his table. The expressions around him said the other guys weren't wild about the idea either.

"Maybe a picture?" Audra was staring at the center of the table as though one might jump out at her. "I'd love a rose. Maybe not a giant one but a branch with several blooms arched across the middle. Pink with green leaves that both had hints of the brown under them to blend with the background. It wouldn't be brown like a plant no one had watered but more like... ethereal... like it's fading into the table. It could..." She stopped talking abruptly as she realized both that she'd drifted into her own world and that no one had followed.

Most of the cards had been dealt and Trevor had already ruled out a Grand Tichu.

"Oh, this is better." Audra grabbed one of the cards from in front of Logan and held it up, pointing at the back. "You could have her paint the table to look like the back of a Tichu deck."

Trevor thought about that for about half a second before he shook his head. "Way too busy," he said. "It's okay on a little card, but if we blow it up to the size of this table, I'd be tired of looking at it pretty quickly."

"It's always about you, isn't it?" Audra teased.

"It's my table."

She smiled. "It wouldn't have to be busy. If you kept most of the surface the natural wood color and painted the symbols with a low contrast color..."

"Can I have my card back?" Logan held out a hand for it.

Audra didn't even look at him as she waited for Trevor to give it another second of thought.

"I still don't like it," he said. "I don't know what any of those symbols mean — if they mean anything — and I'd feel weird about that."

"Just think of it as a pattern."

He made a face at her rather than repeat that he didn't like the idea.

"What about one of the suits?" She flipped the card around to show everyone the three of swords.

"Hey!" Logan snatched it from her hand. "Thanks for showing everyone my card."

Audra only shrugged an apology.

"It's a three," Cameron said. "I predict you're giving that away anyway."

"What about a big black sword in the middle of the table?" Audra suggested. She reached between Logan and Ryan to wave her hand over the proposed location. She still seemed unconcerned that people were trying to play a game.

"Well, I like the sword idea better than the flowers," Ryan said as he passed his cards around Audra.

"Still too much," Trevor said. "Plus, it's like picking a favorite suit, and people don't have a favorite suit."

"I do," Logan said.

"Swords," Cameron said.

They nodded at each other.

"All four of the suits? But smaller." Audra straightened and gasped as an idea hit. "One in each corner," she said. "Just one small symbol on each corner. It would be subtle yet distinctive enough to mark it the official Tichu table."

"I think you're finally on to something," Trevor said. He waved a hand at his sister. "Now back up so we can play some official Tichu."

7

*A*lison recognized the sound of her mother's footsteps behind her. She wasn't surprised by the voice, but she was still unprepared for the question.

"Looking out the window again?"

"Audra should be here any minute," Alison said. That was true. And it was why she was looking out the window. If Audra walked up carrying paintings, she might need someone to open the door for her. A small part of Alison was hoping to see someone else while she watched though. She knew that was what her mom was really asking.

"I know he'll be back," she said, which was the proof.

"Mom, it's been like two weeks. Time to let it go."

"I would if you would."

Alison shook her head in disagreement. She couldn't help that an occasional stray thought made her wonder what he thought of the shop, why he looked familiar, or what had sent him in there for coffee in the first place. Once could be shrugged off as some random occurrence, but twice in a row then never was odd. Wasn't it? Was she only making excuses to think about him? But even with the stray thoughts, she didn't actually expect to see him again, unlike her mom. "I'm watching for Audra," Alison insisted.

"Okay." Her mom answered in a smug tone that said she was willing to drop the subject *for the moment*.

That made it harder for Alison to drop it. "In the incredibly unlikely event that you're right about him coming back, can you do me a favor and be less creepy?"

"How so?" She scrunched up her eyes in fake innocence, as though she didn't understand what would make her daughter ask such a thing.

"Mom, you admitted it was creepy the way you were staring at him the whole time."

"I need to gauge his interest level."

"No, you don't."

She took a deliberately long sip from her mug to delay an answer. "Of course I do," she said eventually. "But I'm sure I can be more subtle about it."

Alison didn't like the way she said it. She spotted Audra out of the corner of her eye, and it wasn't going to happen anyway so she turned away from the annoying conversation to let in their new business associate. Alison was halfway outside before she realized that Audra wasn't alone. Ryan was right behind her holding a painting in each hand.

Alison scrambled to keep all of her scrambling internal and present a calm welcome. "Good morning, Audra. I'm glad to see you found someone to help you carry everything."

"Yeah. I don't really need the muscle, but I'll make fewer trips this way." She stepped inside.

"Morning, Alison," Ryan said.

She smiled and greeted him, though she was slightly unnerved by his expression. He seemed just a little too happy to see her. Was there really some sort of secret crush going on? She did her best to act naturally as she followed them inside and directed them to the side where the paintings would be hung. Alison had let Audra know they would display her work only last night. Audra had been seriously excited – though trying to hide it – and volunteered to bring her work in first thing in the morning. Alison figured that was just as well. It'd be easier to discuss placement in person.

"You can set those on the tables for now, or anywhere else." Alison gestured to a couple of old tables. No worries about getting those scratched.

Audra plopped her pair of paintings face up on the closer table. Ryan held the ones in his hands up for Audra to take. They rattled slightly as they hit the table. Was it extraordinarily considerate of Ryan to let Audra handle her work when she didn't seem overly protective of it? Or was Alison looking for reasons to encourage his interest in her?

He'd never really caught her eye, but he wasn't a bad-looking guy. A little heavy, but he had kind eyes. She took note that they were dark blue, which seemed somehow a good match for the dark blond hair. His jaw didn't sag, which was just a weird thing to notice. Alison mentally slapped herself with a rejoinder to act naturally.

"It was nice of you to lend an extra pair of hands this morning," she said.

Ryan nodded modestly. "It's also nice to have a sister who owes you."

Alison smiled involuntarily. Sense of humor. Check.

Ryan turned to Audra. "She'll owe me more when I have to pay for this later."

"It'll be fine," Audra said, waving off his concern. She clearly understood the meaning behind his cryptic statement though.

"Should I go ahead and bring in the rest while you two discuss where they're going to hang?" Ryan asked.

Audra looked at Alison for any sign of objection before she nodded.

"There's a block near the door you can use to prop it open if you —"

"I'll show him." Alison's mom cut her off and was already moving to follow Ryan to the door.

Alison hadn't realized her mom had followed them from the door. She waved a thanks after her and turned her attention back to Audra. "How do you hang your paintings?"

Audra's eyes darted around uncertainly. "Um…"

"Are there brackets on the back or any particular hardware to make them secure? Or do you just hang them on nails?"

"A nail is fine," Audra said. The excitement that had emitted from her since she arrived faded. "Is that wrong? And are you really okay with me putting a bunch of holes in the wall?"

Alison refrained from asking how she'd thought they were going to display the art and simply tried to reassure her. "You can see we're not going to be ruining smooth drywall or anything. My grandparents wanted a warehouse look." She turned to indicate the rough wood wall. "A few nail holes will hardly be noticeable."

"Your grandparents?" Audra asked. "Is this their store?"

"They opened it, but my grandpa passed away a few years ago and my grandma retired."

"My grandparents own the restaurant next door." Audra tipped her head that direction.

"Cool. I have lunch there sometimes," Alison said. "It's good."

Ryan handed Audra two paintings and turned around again without a word. He barely glanced at Alison. There wasn't anything nervous or awkward in his retreat, only purpose.

"He thinks if he gets out of here fast enough, it'll be like he wasn't here," Audra said. She turned away with her hand going towards her mouth.

Alison thought she might have been turning an invisible key. Did she have more to say that she was reminding herself not to say? How could Ryan be interested in Alison but also interested in spending as little time with her as possible? Had she done something to make him think a relationship would be a bad idea? The thought stung. How could she be ruled out based on greetings they exchanged every few Sundays?

And then Alison remembered that she was not a drama-loving teenager and stopped herself from building an implausible scenario based on what may very well have been Audra scratching her chin. Back to the task at hand. "I have a hammer here and a whole box of nails." Alison pointed to the tools on the floor by the wall. "I'm happy to help you, but if you're okay on your own I can just leave you to decide where you want everything."

Audra bit her lip. "I can use the whole wall? I know you said on the phone that management was giving me a wall, but..." She turned her head to look from one end to the other. The shop was longer than it was wide. "This is a big wall," she said. "I can put paintings anywhere?"

"You can. If it's more space than you need, the last eight or ten feet would probably be best to leave blank. That's where I work, and I might kick up some dust with light sanding or make people walk around a mess to get a better look."

Audra grinned. "Stay out of your space," she interpreted. "I can do that." She surveyed the wall again and appeared more satisfied with a limitation. Probably because she sensed the honesty behind it.

Alison hadn't been intentionally holding back. This was simply new so she was still realizing that she would prefer not to have paintings in her space as she said it. Audra made it sound joking enough they could both smile about it. "Oh, I forgot a level," Alison said. "I'll be right back."

She rushed into the back room where her dad was hugging a large dresser. "Do you need help moving that?" she asked.

"I'm not moving it," he said. "I'm... repositioning it."

Alison didn't laugh as he sounded serious. He was fully engrossed in whatever he was doing and gave her a thanks but no thanks wave. She shrugged and pulled a small level from a drawer.

She stopped the drawer when it was halfway closed and grabbed a tape measure as well. "Paintings are here," she said before she left.

He only grunted in acknowledgement.

When Alison returned, Ryan was walking away again, and Audra was looking between the wall and her growing collection of canvases. The fingers on one hand were skimming the handle of the hammer as though she was itching to pick it up and get to work.

"Do you need some time to plan out where they're going to go?"

Audra nodded. Her eyes remained glued to the wall for a few seconds before she turned back to Alison. "I think I have a good idea, but I want to be sure before I start making holes."

Alison was amused by her continued concern over putting holes in a wall that was designed to look distressed and weathered. Perhaps later she would tell Audra about the time her parents had needed to replace a section and gave Alison and her sisters the job of banging on the new piece to make it match. She did appreciate thinking the job through before she started though. "Well, here's a level," she said as she handed it over.

"Thanks." Audra held it up to watch the bubble float.

"And a tape measure. Is there anything else you think you'll need?"

"Hopefully not band-aids," Audra said. "I admit I have very little experience with all these tools."

Alison laughed. "We do have a first aid kit, but I think it'd be insulting to have it ready."

"You haven't seen me swing a hammer yet."

"I'll be sure to stand back."

Now Audra laughed.

"One thing I know you don't need," Alison said, "is me hovering. I'm going to head over to my little corner to work. Just come get me if you need anything or have any questions."

Audra glanced at Ryan on his way back with more art. "I better get some nails up before we run out of table space."

Alison smiled at both of them before she began walking to the back, still smiling. This collaboration was a good idea. She was more convinced than ever. It was going to be nice to have someone other than her parents hanging around the shop, even if it was only a few hours a week.

Her current project was a small end table. The stain was dry, and Alison had gotten out her paints before Audra arrived. The customer wanted ivy on the doors. Alison believed she was fairly good at drawing before she saw Audra's art. Most of Alison's work was copying though, and she had more confidence in that area. Requests for pictures or designs were almost always to match something the customer already had. She didn't doubt her skills at that.

This request was for ivy that matched a wallpaper border. The customer had left a piece of that paper. Alison could tell the table would be too high to work on from the floor. She tipped it onto its front and set a door on the back with the design she had to copy. She thought it was ugly. Fortunately, her skills at masking her opinions were better than her drawings.

She cast an occasional eye or ear over the shop as she went to work. A young couple came in showing interest in tables. She let them browse in peace. Solo shoppers typically wanted help sooner than groups, who preferred to discuss the furniture out of earshot of the proprietors. Or at least believing they were out of earshot. Alison could hear enough to know that the man thought they needed a smaller table than the woman. There were two other customers that Alison's mom had already offered to help. It would be important to pay closer attention if her mom became busy with any of them. Then Alison became aware of Ryan standing nearby, apparently waiting to be noticed.

"Hey," he said. "I hope this isn't the worst time for an interruption."

She smiled up at him to show that it really wasn't. "Do you or Audra need something?"

"I got all of her pictures inside and was about to take off, but she wanted me to ask you first if it's okay for her to be hammering while there are customers in the store."

"Oh, it'll be fine," Alison assured him. "We work on the furniture here so there's regularly some banging and..." She paused as a loud scraping and growling came from the back room. It sounded as though her dad was "repositioning" that dresser across the concrete floor. "Plus, whatever that was was worse."

Ryan smiled and also looked curious about what had made the noise. He turned away from the door. "I'll let her know," he said. "Take care."

She waved and returned her attention to her first ugly green leaf. She had a vine down the left side and halfway across the top. It matched the vine on her sample so far. She was satisfied despite it being ugly. A tapping noise informed Alison that Audra was committing to her first nail at last as she applied her brush to forming the next leaf. And it was definitely more of a tapping than a banging. There was no reason to think it would be disturbing to anyone. More likely, it would pique their interest in the new addition to the shop.

Though Alison didn't consider the painting difficult, it was time consuming. She had to move the brush very slowly to keep it steady and pause frequently to study what she was copying. By the time she had a few more leaves, it sounded as though Audra had tapped in quite a few nails. Alison decided to check on the progress and give her legs a stretch at the same time.

The painting placement seemed random at first glance. There were seven on the wall. As Alison stepped closer, she could see diagonal rows forming. Audra turned to her with an excited grin. Something expectant in her eyes seemed to be asking for approval.

"This looks great," Alison said. "I love this one." She gestured to the painting with the shadows going towards the sun. Already it was one of her favorites.

"Thanks." Audra held up the level. "I think you've created a monster though."

"How so?"

"I love this." She set it on top of the painting she'd just hung. "I've always just used my eyes to get them as straight as possible and suddenly that's not good enough because I've never thought to use a level. I want one that fits in my pocket so I can pull it out whenever I visit someone who has one of my paintings. I can quickly check the placement. And I'm going to want to use it every time I come here. I'm going to be super annoying making sure these stay straight."

"That's not annoying. It simply shows you care about your work." Alison's mom had joined them. The morning had worn on enough that she'd ditched the coffee mug.

"Thank you," Audra said. She seemed a bit nervous around the older woman. "I appreciate this opportunity to, um, display some of my paintings."

"They are, if I may say, delightfully kooky."

Audra tipped her head modestly to acknowledge the compliment.

"I knew we wanted to work with you as soon as Alison told me your grandfather's word for them. It's what my husband says about the jewelry so it seemed like a good sign." She gestured at the case of sparkly beaded objects.

"He doesn't say it about the jewelry," Alison explained. "He says it about the woman who makes the jewelry. Minus the word delightful."

Audra's eyes widened and her mouth twitched. She seemed to be deciding whether or not to voice a question.

"Sheila and I have been friends since grade school. There was an immediate clash when Jim and I started dating. The animosity has turned almost playful over the years as they've gotten used to each other."

"Dad usually prefers to stay in the back room," Alison added, "but sometimes he comes up front when Sheila is here just to make a show of retreating."

"Oh. Wait." Audra moved a finger between Alison and her mom. "You called her husband Dad so…"

"Oh, my goodness." Alison gave herself a light smack on the forehead. "I forgot to do introductions. This is Audra Norman, our new artist in residence. Audra, this is Elaine Brachy, my mom. My dad's name is Jim. He's the one making weird noises in the back and may pop out to meet you at some point."

The two women smiled at each other while Alison formally introduced them. Then her mom said, "I wanted to ask if you're related to May Norman."

"My grandmother."

"That's what I thought."

Alison crinkled her forehead. Did she know May Norman? She thought her mom had mentioned the name May but without a last name.

"I wonder if I should have made the connection sooner," Audra said. "Since you said your grandparents first started the business." She addressed Alison's mom. "Would that be your parents or your husband's?"

"Mine," she said. "They hired Jim my last year of high school. He had just graduated. He's worked here nearly as long as I have."

Audra gave a mushy smile. "So that's how you two met?"

"Yep. I had a crush on him immediately, but it was over a year before he asked me out. He said later he was afraid he'd lose his job if things didn't work out. The blessing of this place couldn't be ignored forever though."

Alison rolled her eyes. "Here we go again," she said.

"What?" Audra asked eagerly.

The expression on her face showed that Alison's mom relished the chance to explain her insane idea to someone new. "After the shop brought me and Jim together, God used it to find husbands for all three of our daughters."

"All three?" Audra turned to Alison in shock. "You're married?"

Alison shook her head as she tried to process the shock. Had there been something in their conversations that contradicted the news? Was she concerned for Ryan? Or should Alison be offended that the idea of her having a husband was generally shocking?

"Not yet," her mom clarified.

"Oh, but you're..." Audra's eyes dropped, possibly in search of an engagement ring.

Alison thought it best to take over the explanation before her mom threw in too many details, like anything that sounded like she was pining over a certain guy who liked coffee. "My mom is convinced that one of our recent customers will eventually marry me based *entirely* on a pattern that she's manufactured in her head."

Her mom smiled indulgently rather than insert her version so Alison continued. "Yes, my parents met here and my oldest sister Angela did in fact meet her husband when he came in here with his brothers to pick out a new dining room table for an anniversary gift for their parents. He kept coming back to check on the progress and ask kind of stupid questions about the table after it was delivered, and it's actually a sweet story. But my other sister, Amanda... her husband already knew her from school and came in here deliberately to talk to her. That doesn't count as meeting here, and it certainly doesn't prove that I will be so lucky."

Audra's smile was flickering. She seemed very interested and eager for more information but hesitant to ask. Alison's mom had something in her dark eyes that looked a little like gloating, as though

Alison had somehow made her point by explaining how she didn't have a point. Alison decided they needed to get to a safer subject immediately. If they continued with this theory, one of two bad things would happen. Either she would accidentally mention that she wished the coffee guy would come back. Or Ryan's name would come up.

"Let's talk about your paintings instead," she said.

Both of the other women laughed at the obvious subject change.

Then Alison's mom got more serious. "Yes, let's talk about how none of them are framed."

It only took a second for Audra to catch on, and her eyes lit up at the prospect of the arrangement being mutually beneficial.

Trevor sat in his car with the air conditioner at full blast. The drive had been short enough that the air had just gotten cool. He wanted to build up some defense against the July afternoon sun. The store was only half a block away, but that would be enough time for the heat to make him look as nervous as he felt.

It was possible he was nuts to even think he could make up for the bad impressions. He didn't have anything to lose. That wasn't why he was going to try though. He was going to talk to Alison again simply because he wanted to talk to her. Also, he might go insane thinking about her if he didn't.

When he'd been hit with enough air that he was nearly shivering, he shut off the car and walked with purpose towards the store he hadn't even noticed a few weeks ago. He pulled open the door with just the right amount of force. No knocking himself over or tripping over the threshold. So far so good. The inside was different than he remembered, and he immediately saw why. Those were Audra's paintings all over the wall. Already?

She'd texted that it was going to happen. There had been a lot of exclamation points and smiley faces but no details. She must have been in that morning. Why hadn't she asked him to help? It being morning probably answered his question so a better one was why hadn't she waited? It would have been the perfect opportunity to...

"Hello!"

Trevor turned to the woman who had approached while he was distracted by the paintings. Was this the same woman who had greeted him the last two times? Her hair was brown. It wasn't brown and gray like the first time or the awful straw color, just brown. It might have been a little shorter, too. Did she change her hair every day to confuse people or what?

"Are you looking for something in particular?" she asked. A strange smile hinted there was something funny about the question. He could have sworn the woman was trying not to wiggle her eyebrows at him.

Now he was feeling a little trapped. Trevor's plan was to browse until he could determine if Alison was there, then ask her about the table. The creepy woman made him want to establish a legitimate reason for being in the store as soon as possible. He trusted he could figure out a way to get Alison's input on the project soon. "I have an old table at home," he said. "It's not in very good shape, and I wondered if I could talk to someone here about fixing it up for me."

The woman appeared to be thinking. Was she thinking about sending him to Alison for help? She had done that before.

"How old is the table?" she asked.

He shrugged. "I really don't know. My grandmother gave it to me. She was already calling it the old table when I was a kid."

"Was it her idea for you to have it refinished?" The woman smiled. She seemed overeager for information that didn't have anything to do with getting it fixed.

"She gave it to me a few years ago," he said. "It was my idea." But even as he protested, there was a vague memory of Grandma May mentioning that table while he was drinking his coffee earlier in the week. She'd only asked him if he still had it, but he'd been thinking about Alison then. Maybe Grandma May had inadvertently given him the idea. It still wasn't important. Trevor needed to focus on finding someone – he hopefully scanned the back of the store – to talk to about the idea, regardless of where it came from.

The woman had nothing in her hands in the afternoon, no white coffee mug. She waved one of those free hands for him to follow. "Come with me," she said. "We'll talk details."

Trevor followed her about three-quarters the length of the shop. They quickly passed the nicer furniture and entered the sea of rough wood. Was she going to try to sell him a different table? She turned around somewhat suddenly. "Is this a coffee table or full-size dining?"

"Uh… it's a small kitchen table. Four-person. It's great for card games."

"Is it structurally sound?"

"I don't believe it's in any danger of falling apart," he said, not sure how to answer the question.

"Does it have any loose or wobbling legs, warped or splintered wood, things like that?" she asked. "Or does it just need cosmetic work?"

"The latter."

She nodded and seemed to be waiting for something.

Trevor glanced around, wondering why they needed to move over here to have the conversation. Had they been blocking the doorway? He heard the humming of some sort of machine from the back room. Was that Alison?

Just as the silence began to get uncomfortable, the woman took a step forward and lowered her voice. "I'm going to have you talk directly to Alison about this." She tipped her head towards the back, and then walked away.

Trevor was somewhat dumbfounded. Why had she started asking questions if she wanted him to talk to someone else? Was he supposed to walk into the back room, right past the "employees only" sign? Well, he wanted to talk to Alison, and it seemed he'd been given permission to do that.

He weaved back to the center aisle thinking of intelligent words to use. Scuffed and scratched, not beat up. Refinish, not fix. He could mention that it was not structurally unsound. He was looking towards the back door and didn't realize Alison wasn't behind it until he nearly walked right past her. She was sitting on the floor, hidden from farther away by a large armoire. "Hi," he said.

She was visibly startled. The paintbrush Trevor hadn't noticed in her hand slipped. "Hello," she said as she put it down. She picked up a rag, dipped a corner in a small can and wiped away the smudge he'd caused.

"I'm so sorry," Trevor said. "I didn't mean to sneak up on you."

"No real harm." She put down the rag and moved to stand up as she said, "What can I help you with?"

He continued to study the little cabinet she was painting. "Every time I come in here, you're working on something different. You must have a lot of skills."

"It's my job," she answered with a modest shrug.

"You're good at it," he said. "Those leaves are…" Ugly. The leaves were actually very ugly. But they were perfect copies of the ones on the paper, and that's what impressed him. "You just drew those free hand?"

Alison raised an arm and nodded towards the wall where Audra's paintings were hanging. "You should check out our new additions if you want to admire real art."

Seeing the work reminded him of his sister, the one who told Alison he was obsessed with her and annoyed him by not letting him help bring in the paintings and who knew what else she'd said that morning. It seemed a light tone was the best way to avoid or at least lessen some awkwardness. "I wouldn't call that real art," he said.

"Really? You wouldn't say she's probably the most talented artist in town?"

"That's definitely not something I want to go on record as saying," he said with a laugh. He expected Alison to laugh with him, thought in fact that she'd set him up for the joke. But she sort of looked... offended?

"I love those pictures," she said.

She sounded so serious. Was she about to say "gotcha" or did she really not understand how it worked with siblings? "Do you have any siblings?" he asked.

Her eyes crinkled at the question. "I have two sisters. Both older. I think I heard something about a table you want refinished."

Trevor followed her to the new subject still not sure what happened to the last one. "Yes," he said. "I have an old table, a hand-me-down from my grandparents, that I'd like refinished. If that's something you do. I mean, I know you *can*, but... do you only work on pieces you've acquired yourself?"

Alison shook her head and looked a moment longer at something that caught her eye off to the side. It made her silky brown ponytail come forward and rest on her shoulder. "Does it need any other work?"

"No." The hair was perfect. But she meant his table. "Yes. But not... it isn't wobbly or anything, but I wondered if you could paint some suits on the edges."

"Suits?"

"Like cards," he said. Movement over her shoulder told him what she might have noticed a minute ago. The woman who had greeted Trevor at the door was dusting furniture nearby. Too nearby to be coincidental. She got to the corner of a dresser and rather than move around it, she moved to the next piece so that she was still facing Trevor and Alison.

"You mean like a heart on one side, a club on another and so on?"

"Not exactly," Trevor said. "We mostly play a game called Tichu. Have you ever heard of it?"

She shook her head.

Trevor was ready for that and pulled out his phone to show her some pictures. "It has different suits than a standard deck of cards. They look like this."

She leaned closer to see the pictures, and he caught a hint of cocoa butter or something that reminded him of the beach before she leaned back with a nod. "Those look fairly simple. I should be able to draw them. Where do you... or how big do you want them?"

"Over here." Trevor motioned towards a table a short distance away. He didn't need a visual, but it wouldn't hurt and the creepy woman was running her dustrag over something she'd already dusted. An excuse to move away from her didn't hurt either. The table was rectangular instead of square like his. It was the beveled edge he planned to use as an example though. He paused in his head to appreciate that he knew the word beveled. That would be a good one to use out loud. "My table has an edge just like this, and I was thinking I'd like to put a row of the four Tichu suits on the right side of each bevel."

Alison smiled. It was possible she liked his idea. It was also possible she was amused that he'd used bevel as a noun when it might not be a noun. Was it a noun? It seemed, however, that she was actually amused by something behind him.

Trevor lowered his voice. "Did she follow us?"

"You noticed, huh?" Alison seemed to be struggling between amused and annoyed. She mumbled something that seemed to end with the word subtle.

"Does the creepy woman spy on you a lot?" he asked, still trying to keep his voice quiet.

"I think she's spying on *you*." She seemed entertained by the thought and checking for his reaction to it.

"Does she think I might try to stuff this table in my pocket and walk out with it or something?"

Alison had a pretty laugh, possibly in part because she now seemed entertained by Trevor and not the woman. He tried to keep it up with a conspiratorial whisper. "Do you think I could get away with it?"

She was still smiling as she said, "I think if you could get that in your pocket, then I probably couldn't stop you."

Trevor grabbed the edge of the table as though he might try to pick it up. "Now I'm tempted to try."

"To try to get me in trouble with management?" She looked totally serious as her eyes flicked to his hands and back up.

He was confused. "For letting me try to put a table in my pocket?"

"For letting you get fingerprints all over our merchandise."

Trevor pulled his hands back. The furniture around them – including that particular table – was used and definitely not shiny, but maybe the creepy woman was still intent on keeping it clean. Before he could get out an apology, Alison cracked a smile.

"I'm kidding," she said. "Let's get some details on your project so I can give you an estimate. How big is the table?"

"Thirty-four inches on each side." He was happy both that he'd thought to measure and that he remembered the measurement.

"How tall?"

He hadn't measured that. "Um…"

She waved away the question. "Are there any designs carved into the legs or is the wood pretty flat?"

"Flat," he said, but he heard the hint of uncertainty. Trevor didn't spend much time studying the table's legs. They held it up and didn't wobble. That was all that mattered.

"I don't suppose you have a picture?"

He shook his head. He'd meant to bring a picture. How had he forgotten?

"Okay. I can only give you a range when I haven't seen for myself how much work it will need," she said. And then she gave an estimate.

"That sounds reasonable," Trevor said with a nod.

Alison tilted her head as she regarded him.

It appeared that she could tell he had no idea what anyone else might charge for the same work and therefore had no idea whether it was reasonable or not. He only knew it was a price he was willing to pay. That made it reasonable enough.

"Well," she said after a minute, "if you decide to bring it in, I'll get more specifics about those suits and the stain color and such. I should be able to tell you how long it will take then, too."

"Okay," Trevor said. He felt dismissed. For now. He'd finished what he came for and had permission to come back with a table. "I'll see you again soon."

She smiled as he turned to leave and did not look horrified at the prospect of him returning. Maybe that was progress. Some other customers had come in, and the other woman was talking to them as they opened and closed drawers on a dresser. She spared him a quick wink as he passed that wasn't the least bit creepy. For a moment, he felt as though they were in cahoots about something.

The feeling gave him something to puzzle over as he stepped outside. He was already wondering when he should come back again. Trevor made it nearly to his car before he kicked himself so hard he had to stop walking to do it properly. Alison had said she'd see him when he brought in the table. How exactly was he supposed to bring the table?

It wouldn't fit in his car. He didn't know anyone with a truck. Maybe someone at work but no one he wanted to approach for a favor. He couldn't carry it. Well, he probably lived less than two miles away. It would be physically possible for him to carry the table all the way to the store. But he'd arrive dripping and smelly and would likely endure a few taunts and questions along the way.

Trevor turned around. Surely a place couldn't sell furniture without some way to deliver it. And surely asking Alison to pick up the table wouldn't cost more than trying to rent a truck. At least not in money. It was going to cost his ego to go back in and admit he hadn't realized something so obvious. It had to be done. He strode forward. Another customer entered ahead of him, and Trevor caught the door just before it closed.

The older woman was still helping the same people, but she called out a greeting to the man who entered ahead of Trevor. She said nothing to him though she smiled to see him. The other man went immediately to something he must have seen through the window. Trevor didn't see Alison so he headed towards the back where he'd interrupted her earlier.

She was sitting on the floor again. Trevor approached quietly. He didn't want to startle her again. He stayed back, waiting to be noticed, and watched her hand form a precise curve along the edge of a new leaf. A tiny stroke connected it to the vine. She swished her brush, wiped it on a rag, and dipped it in a lighter shade of green. It hovered in the air for a moment while she measured with her eyes the pattern that was her guide. Then a tiny shake caused a drip of paint to land next to the leaf. "You again?" she said, grabbing a rag.

He'd messed up her work again. "I'm sorry," he said. "I was deliberately trying to stay out of your way."

"Deliberately trying to sneak up on me."

"No, I..." He'd gotten so absorbed in watching her work he'd taken a few steps almost hoping to go unnoticed, which wasn't quite the same as sneaking up on her.

"Never mind." Alison had already cleaned up the drip and was getting to her feet. She plastered on a smile. "I guess you forgot something. Did you have another question?"

"Yes. Would it be possible for you to come and pick up the table? I don't have a truck."

She nodded, slowly. "Yeah. Um, yeah. I... What time of day works for you?"

"I get off work at five, and I'm home a few minutes after that."

"We close at six," she said. "We could stop and get it right after that if you wouldn't be in the middle of dinner or something."

He shook his head and bit his tongue against an impulse to suggest she could join him. Way too pushy.

"Tuesday?" she asked.

"Okay."

"Do you live in the Founder's Mansion?"

Trevor felt his eyes widen. How in the world did she know where he lived?

Alison winced and her eyes darted guiltily to the paintings on the wall.

Of course. Audra had been there. Trevor decided it was best to confirm and get out before either of them had a chance to think too much about anything else Audra had said. "Yes," he said. "Apartment C. You'll come for the table a few minutes after six on Tuesday?"

She nodded, clearly a bit uncomfortable.

"See you soon." Trevor focused on the thought that he would see her again as he made a beeline for the exit.

9

Next Love had a fairly busy Saturday. It was never crowded, but they had at least one customer in the shop the entire afternoon. A few of them lingered over Audra's art. Near the end of the day, an older woman tried to buy a painting. She was standing right next to the sign that said the paintings were only for sale when the artist was present. Alison politely explained the situation without asking if the woman had read the sign. That was partly because she'd seen her read it right before she asked to buy one anyway.

Then the small gray-haired woman demanded that the painting be put back for her. Alison hadn't discussed that eventuality with Audra. She offered to put a little reserved sign under the painting, which appeased the woman. As soon as she had a chance, she texted Audra to let her know how she'd handled it and to expect a customer first thing the next Saturday. Audra's reply came across ecstatic so she apparently approved.

The steady stream of customers was good for several reasons. The first was the most obvious, customers were always good for a business. The second was that it distracted Alison from her thoughts. The third was that since either she or her mom were talking to other people at any given time, they hadn't talked to each other.

Alison loved her mom of course and didn't normally relish being unable to speak to her. But she knew her mom would want to talk about all the thoughts Alison was trying not to think. She was still confused about her interest in that coffee guy. It was weird how he'd insulted the artwork, completely without guile, as though it was okay to joke about someone else's hard work. His reaction to her mom's lack of subtlety was strangely endearing because she'd expected him to pretend he hadn't noticed. She'd almost wondered if asking her to work on a project was a ruse, but he seemed sincere about wanting the work done.

Closing the shop was mostly a matter of turning off the lights and locking the doors, which didn't leave room for much chatting. They were finally alone at home. It was Alison's turn to make dinner. Her dad had disappeared to get cleaned up, and her mom was watching Alison watch water boil.

"When are you going to see him next?"

"Tuesday."

Laughter was the response.

"What's so funny?" Alison asked.

"You knew who I was talking about."

Alison sighed, regretting her quick answer.

"How did things go between you two this afternoon?"

"How did things go?" Alison arched a brow at her mom. "He came in to talk about a table, and you sound like you're asking about a date."

"I'm asking about progress towards a date."

"None," Alison said simply.

"I tried to help."

"How?" Alison set down the box of pasta she'd been about to open.

"I brought him within earshot to talk about his project so you could show some interest. Guys need a little encouragement."

Alison turned away to rip open the box. She'd been surprised, and slightly annoyed, that her mom seemed to be helping the guy herself after all the times she'd insisted he'd be back. Her mind had been on that and not her surroundings, which was why he'd been able to sneak up on her. Her mom's plan had definitely not helped. How was Alison supposed to know she'd been expected to interrupt?

"I did notice," her mom continued, "that the two of you were laughing about something. That looked promising."

"We were actually laughing at the creepy woman spying on us."

Her mom laughed at that. "I guess I helped after all."

"Maybe a little." Alison decided to go ahead and be honest about what was making her grumpy. "That part was kind of... I thought he might be flirting with me so... but then I really messed everything up when he came back."

"How so?" She put her elbows on the counter and leaned forward. "I hoped he'd decided to come back to ask you out."

Alison rolled her eyes. "Not even close. He managed to startle me again." Because she'd been replaying the best parts of their conversation, but there was no need to be quite that honest. "I was kind of embarrassed about that. Then he said he needed someone to pick up the table. I couldn't believe I forgot to ask that, and I got flustered and accidentally revealed that I know where he lives."

"How do you know where he lives?"

"Same building as Audra," she said. "I just happened to see him when I went to check out the paintings."

"Interesting. You didn't tell me about that."

Alison shrugged. "Nothing to tell. I didn't talk to him or anything."

"What makes you think that messed everything up?"

"It got awkward fast," Alison said. "He couldn't get away fast enough. And because I didn't need to get an address from him, I didn't get *any* information, like his name."

"The boy hasn't even introduced himself yet?" Her mom shook her head, probably thinking the wedding would have to be postponed now. Instead of lamenting her faulty expectations though, she said, "His name is Trevor."

The noodles splashed into the pan a bit faster than Alison intended. Fortunately, she managed to avoid burning her arm. "How do you know his name?"

"I have ways of knowing things," her mom said, trying to inject a mysterious tone.

Alison ignored the attempt at mystique. The guy – Trevor, it seemed – must have introduced himself to her mom when he first entered the shop that day. Alison couldn't hear much of the conversation when they were by the door, despite her efforts.

While she was happy to learn the guy's name – Trevor, not "the guy" – she almost wished she didn't know. If he introduced himself to her mom and not to her, there was a teeny tiny chance that was because she made him nervous. She'd been trying to talk herself into giving up hope where he was concerned. But if she made him nervous… the idea was really bad. It could mean she did have a chance. If she went over there to pick up his table thinking she had any chance at all, she'd be more nervous herself, more nervous and flustered and likely to screw up again.

****

Alison drove towards the Founder's Mansion nervous and thinking she was likely to screw up again. It didn't help that her dad was with her. He hadn't said a word about Trevor, or otherwise acted aware of his existence. Alison's mom, however, had said more than a few words to him. She pulled Alison aside just before they left to let her know that he'd been instructed that it was very important for him to orchestrate a few minutes for Trevor and Alison to talk to each other alone.

The truck stopped at the curb with a jittery young woman and a man who had a strong desire to avoid any matchmaking scheme but who was under orders from his wife to be involved in a matchmaking scheme. They had a simple task of picking up a table.

Alison didn't picture it going simply or well. She was a bit of a wreck even without whatever help her dad might grudgingly provide.

Mostly she was obsessing over the name and whether or not he remembered if he'd told it to her. She wasn't going to seem very friendly if she avoided using his name if he thought he'd given it to her. But if she called him Trevor while he was kicking himself for not saying it, she'd be branded a crazy stalker no matter what happened next. No mysterious smile or innocent explanation would save her after she'd already inexplicably known where he lived.

Alison's dad reached the door first and pounded impatiently.

Maybe he just knocked. Alison was looking at the doorbell, thinking they should take their time in pressing it. When her dad skipped right past the button, he seemed to her to be in an awful hurry. Why was he in such a hurry to face the guy when she was trying to wrap her tongue around a greeting that included his name without sounding like she was trying to ask if she was supposed to know that? She'd convinced herself he'd think he told her. Probably.

Her dad stuck out his hand as the door opened. "Jim Brachy from Next Love furniture," he said.

"Ryan Norman."

Ryan!? Alison was at an angle where she saw only a hand extended at first, then all of Ryan appeared in the doorway. What was he doing there? Did he know Trevor? Was he there because he knew Alison was on her way? Oh, no. She didn't know how likely that was, but she knew the possibility gave her something else, something potentially worse, to obsess over.

"We're here to pick up a table," her dad said with a nod to the side to include Alison.

"Come on in," Ryan said. "Hi, Alison."

Alison smiled at the greeting as he stepped back to allow first her dad then her into the apartment. Like Audra's section, the inside was plainer than the outside. White walls, beige carpet, no fancy or old-fashioned light fixtures. Unlike Audra's place, there was no art covering the room. There was a really big TV and a pair of mismatched though very comfortable-looking recliners. One of the chairs had a red blanket tossed over the back. It was too bunched up to be sure, but it might have been a giant Ohio State logo. There was also a table near the front of the room that would be in the way if that was its regular location.

Trevor popped out of a hallway. "Hey, Alison." He nodded at her dad.

"That's Trevor," Ryan said.

At least he was useful. Ryan was talking to her dad, but he'd easily solved the problem of whether or not she should know Trevor's name. She just smiled at him while he shook hands with her dad, who ran his hand over the table as soon as he let go. Then he tried to shake it. Alison hoped that was the right table.

"This is the one you want refinished?" she asked.

"Yeah, that's the one," Trevor said. "I asked my grandma, and she thought it was more than fifty years old."

Alison nodded.

Her dad stood up. He'd been looking under it. "Seems solid," he said with a grunt. He slapped some paperwork on it for Trevor to sign, then he pointed at Ryan. "You help me load it. Alison needs to talk to Trevor."

Flames leapt to Alison's face. She *needed* to talk to Trevor? Was that her dad's idea of delicately arranging a few private words? No. She began to calm down as she realized that it was not. His mind was on the task at hand, which she had a legitimate need to discuss with Trevor.

"Right," she said. She slid the bag on her shoulder down to her elbow where she could root through it and hopefully hide her embarrassment. "I need to have you choose a color and make sure I know exactly what you want on those card symbols."

She had taken a few steps from the door while she spoke to be out of the way of the guys moving the table. Trevor had followed her lead. When she glanced up, he seemed very close. He was still a few feet away and no closer than he'd been when they talked at the shop. But being on his turf made the space somehow smaller, more intimate. It made her hands sweaty.

"Choose a color?" he repeated.

"For the finish." Alison handed him a ring of wood samples from her bag and tried to make sure their fingers didn't touch. Although, it was August. If he seemed to notice how warm she was, she could have pointed out that it was August.

Trevor flipped through the pieces on the ring with an adorably helpless expression. It was almost as though he'd been asked to choose whether he liked his mom or his dad better. His eyes lifted with apology behind them. "These are all different?" he asked.

Some of them were very similar, and he wasn't the first person to point that out. He was the first person to sound as though he was about to get yelled at for thinking they were similar. It made Alison laugh and relax a little. "There's no wrong answer here," she said. "Pick whatever you like, even if it looks a lot like another one."

His expression stiffened. It appeared that being laughed at solidified his doubts and gave him a backbone to defend them. Or maybe just incentive. "Some of these are... Now this one is clearly darker than this one. And this is more of a reddish brown. But these two?" He held the samples up so that two were side by side. "You're telling me these aren't exactly the same?"

"The one on the right, my right, has some orange tint to it."

Trevor squinted at them, then he squinted at her as though he expected a punchline. After a pause, he flipped to two more. "What about these two?"

"This one," she pointed, "has a bit more of the natural wood showing through."

"I don't know what to pick," he said.

"Well… a lot of people like their furniture to match. Are there chairs that go with it, or some other wood in the room you could hold them against? Something you like?"

He turned away, presumably towards his kitchen, with the expression of someone lost in thought. Alison was aware of Ryan and her dad finally getting the table outside and closing the door behind them. She was aware of being alone with a guy she found attractive yet puzzling. Part of her wanted to picture him at a candlelight dinner and part of her wanted to picture him under an interrogation lamp.

"I like the table the way it is," Trevor said. An almost horrified look crossed his face before he began to hastily clarify. "I mean, I do want you to… You've seen the table. It's old. It really needs work. But… can you fix up the scuffs and scratches without really changing it?"

"Sort of. The finish is much more worn in the center than around the edges so giving it a uniform coat will change the overall appearance to a degree even if it's exactly the same as any current spots."

Trevor nodded. "That makes sense. Can you do that?"

"All right." Alison pulled out a notebook to jot down his preference. She wasn't going to forget what he said, but she was in the habit of writing down all customer requests. It felt more professional to have a record. She would need notes for the next part anyway. "Let's talk about the, um, the cards you mentioned."

"Tichu," Trevor said. "It's a great game. I play every week with a few friends. Of course, I eat at the table more often. But it used to belong to my grandparents, and it was… it was used for games, kind of like it wasn't good enough for meals even though…" His eyes seemed to refocus on the present. "You just want to know where to put the symbols, not the life story of the table."

"That's okay. It's interesting," she said, which was about the least interesting thing *she* could have said. She took the ring of samples from him without adding any other dull comments.

Trevor seemed to sense a lack of interest as he pulled a deck of cards from his pocket and stripped off a rubber band. "These are the suits," he said, fanning out the cards to show the faces. "There are four. I'd like a row of them on the right side of each edge."

Alison got her notebook ready. "What order?"

"I'm not... uh... maybe a different order on each side?"

She held her pen ready to list some possible arrangements but paused as she considered what to write. She wasn't going to try to sketch those shapes in front of Trevor and didn't know what to call them. Descriptive names might be as embarrassing as calling regular suits clovers or shovels. But these were all different colors. "We have blue, red, black and green," she said. "There are more than four possible orders. Which ones do you want?"

He shrugged. "As random as possible. Except swords, or black, should be first on at least one side."

"Why?"

"Apparently some people have favorite suits."

Alison laughed because his tone said that was silly, but she liked the blue suit best. Even though it looked the most difficult to draw. "Okay. Give me four random orders."

He began to name the suits – by color, thankfully – even though he clearly thought choosing himself was unnecessary.

Alison dutifully copied down his lists. She preferred specific instructions, and she already let him get away with leaving the finish somewhat vague. "Once I have the table ready except for the decoration, I'll take a picture and put these on the picture digitally for you to approve the size and placement before I put them on the actual table."

Trevor nodded, though he looked as though he thought that was also unnecessary.

"Do you want me to send the picture by text or email or…" She trailed off to let him fill in the blank.

"Text is fine."

"Your number?"

He recited it.

Alison read through her notes to see if she had any other questions. The one thing she still wanted to ask Trevor was if he would be interested in talking about something other than his table sometime. Her mother's voice suddenly echoed in her head, telling her that guys needed encouragement, suggesting that she should offer to let him come check on her progress whenever he wanted. She stuffed her notebook back in her bag and grabbed some courage along with a business card. "That has my number on it," she said. "If you want to ask me about the progress or… anything else, that would be okay. I'll see if they have it loaded."

She turned to the door before she could see his reaction to being handed the card. Why had she done that now? She was still going to have to talk to him to deliver the table. It would have been less awkward to wait until their business association was over.

Trevor followed her outside. They were just in time to see her truck bounce as Ryan jumped off the back. Her dad looked satisfied and already held her passenger door open for his getaway.

"Thanks for your help," she said to Ryan.

"No problem," he said. He was walking towards Trevor.

She waved to both of them.

They smiled at her at the same time, and it was the same smile. She noticed several other similarities, too. The shape of their eyes, the slope of their noses, the reason Trevor had looked so familiar when she first met him. He reminded her of Ryan. Alison's feet stopped midstep. "Hey. Are you guys related?"

"We're brothers," Ryan said. They both seemed surprised by the question.

Now that she saw the resemblance, she figured they were surprised it took her so long to ask. "Oh, uh… bye." Alison waved again and hurried to her truck. The new information gave her the weird feeling that she was missing something.

10

*T*revor and Ryan walked around the building to Audra's apartment. They were letting her host the week's Tichu game since Trevor was temporarily without a table. Ryan, because he lived in the same place, didn't have a table either. Cameron had a table and a roommate who worked nights, and they didn't want to play in silence. Logan lived with his parents and a younger brother and sister who would want to play.

Ryan pushed the doorbell, and they waited.

"Hi," Audra said as she let them in.

"Did you see what we did there?" Trevor asked.

She stopped, looking confused. "What?"

"How we rang the doorbell, then waited for you to answer? That's how a doorbell works."

She just rolled her eyes and continued into the room. "Logan's already here."

That was obvious as Logan was sitting on the couch with Audra's roommate, Violet. He nodded greetings while she offered the new arrivals a big smile. Violet had dark curly hair that was usually pinned up in a mass at the back of her head with spirals dangling from it. It was pretty, but Trevor always spent a moment wondering how she did it. And noticing how it seemed the opposite of his sister's light blonde hair that usually hung straight down.

Alison's hair was somewhere in the middle, a lighter shade of brown, only slightly wavy, and so far tucked back in a simple ponytail. Neither Violet nor Audra's hair was too anything, but he still enjoyed the thought of Alison's being just right.

"Audra says she sold a painting already," Logan said.

Trevor looked at her. "I thought you were only selling them on Saturdays."

"Thanks for the congratulations," Audra said. She plopped onto her couch between Logan and Violet.

"Congratulations," Trevor said, "but when did this happen?"

"Well, it hasn't exactly happened yet." Audra sounded more defensive than sheepish. "Technically I'm selling them whenever the store is open since they're always on display but... Anyway, Alison told me someone really liked one and plans to come first thing tomorrow to buy it."

"She probably won't be the only one," Logan said.

Ryan nodded.

Trevor felt his phone buzz. He was happy for the distraction, otherwise he might have been tempted to explain that he'd have been happier for Audra and the interest in her work if she hadn't tried to exaggerate it. Or was that Logan? Trevor was happy until he read the text. "Cameron is having some sort of car trouble and has to walk. He'll be about fifteen minutes late."

"I'll pick him up." Ryan moved towards the door before anyone could stop him.

Trevor didn't think too hard about volunteering to go instead, but he might have if he'd known what was coming.

Audra leaned forward like a pirate examining the booty. "Now's my chance to ask if you've made any progress with Alison."

"I heard there was a new love interest," Violet said with a smile.

Trevor frowned at them discussing his life like some sort of rom com. He knew Audra though. If he denied anything or refused to talk about it, she'd only bug him more. Of course, that didn't mean he planned to go into detail. "She picked up the table on Tuesday, as planned."

"And?" Audra prompted.

"And I picked a color for the finish." He'd sort of picked a color.

"And?" Audra widened her eyes and waved her hand impatiently.

Trevor didn't think there was anything left to say.

"Sparks were flying?" Violet tried. Then she paused to consider if that was the expression she wanted. They all knew what she meant anyway.

"I don't know," Logan said. "Sounds like she didn't even know he existed."

The girls laughed, but Trevor didn't understand the joke.

"She didn't know Ryan had a brother," he explained.

That wasn't the same as not knowing he existed, and it wasn't funny. They knew that, too, so he let them have their laugh. It was short.

"Seriously though," Audra said. "Any hope?"

Trevor shrugged. Of course he had hope. He would hope until Alison explicitly took it away. But his sister likely meant to ask if he had a reason to hope. A shrug was the best answer.

"Don't blow me off," Audra said. "I'm being supportive." A gleam in her eye said she was supportive *and* nosy.

"I really don't know." Trevor was tired of being the only one standing. It felt like a spotlight. He took a seat in an armchair that looked a lot more comfortable than it was. It was old, and the springs bent too far under his weight.

Audra and Violet shared a significant look. It didn't have anything to do with the popping noises that came from the chair. They were used to that. Violet nodded. "If you don't know, that means she said or did something you don't know how to interpret. Let's hear it."

That seemed like an incredible leap to Trevor. She was right, but it was still a leap. When was Ryan going to get back with Cameron so they could play the game he was there to play? He glanced at Logan, who was clearly not going to be any help. He just sat there.

"Come on. Out with it." Audra grinned eagerly at Violet, even though she was talking to Trevor. "What happened? We'll help you figure it out."

He sighed. "Let's say, hypothetically, you were talking to a guy about a... some sort of business thing. And you gave him your phone number because it made sense in that context. But you said it would be okay to call about anything else. Could that be a hint or do you mean only anything else related to the business thing, and it only came out sort of overly polite, maybe?"

"What did she say exactly?" Audra asked.

"Just what I said."

"Well, how did she word it?"

"I..."

He couldn't answer before Violet said, "How she said it is more important than what she said."

"Oh, yes," Audra agreed. "Did it sound like a hint?"

Trevor shrugged again. "Kind of. But I'm afraid I only heard what I wanted to hear."

"Were you obvious about that?" Audra glanced at Violet again, as though she would know.

Violet nodded and seemed to know something.

Trevor looked between them. "What does that have to do with anything?"

"If you were acting interested, she'd be on her guard against any accidental encouragement," Audra explained.

"I bet he was obvious," Violet said.

Fortunately, Ryan and Cameron returned before Trevor was asked to analyze the encounter further. The examination went on in his head regardless. Had he been obvious? He'd tried to avoid that because he hadn't wanted to make her uncomfortable, but had he succeeded? It was possible she picked up on the interest and intended to hint that it was welcome. And it was possible that she didn't and was thinking only of questions regarding the table. Even after his sister had tried to help, he was still stuck trying to read Alison's mind.

*A*lison's mind was drifting again, drifting to Trevor, wondering when he might call to ask about the table. She had no idea what she'd say when he did. She hadn't started it. Why had she been in such a hurry to pick up his table when she already had several other pieces in line?

She knew why. But she couldn't tell Trevor she'd been so eager to work with him that she hadn't thought about anything else, like her other customers or the fact that he might be without a table for a while. She felt as though she was now holding it hostage until Trevor called her.

But maybe he had another table. And maybe he wasn't as eager as she hoped. Alison had a long and growing list of questions about Trevor. It had been difficult to keep it all quiet when she spent the morning with a woman she now knew was his sister. The knowledge answered some questions but raised others. It explained Trevor joking about the quality of Audra's paintings. It did not explain why he thought she would understand the joke. He'd never mentioned his sister, or anyone else in his family, or much about himself at all.

The more Alison tried to tell herself to stop being curious, the more curious she felt. Mostly about Audra's comment that her brother was obsessed. It took on a new light now that Alison knew she had more than one brother. Alison also felt annoyed. For thinking about Trevor so much. With her mom, for occasionally asking pretend innocent questions they both knew would make her think of Trevor. And with Trevor, because obviously it was all somehow his fault.

And she was annoyed at the woman who had insisted on the reserved sign on one of Audra's paintings and hadn't shown up to claim it. At least that had given them something to talk about whenever Alison considered asking Audra about her brother. That was a juvenile temptation that she needed to resist. It shouldn't have been difficult so she was kind of mad at herself for being grateful they were both too busy for more than brief chats anyway. While no one actually purchased one of the paintings, plenty of people showed interest and wanted to talk to Audra about them. Alison, of course, had to finish her project so she could get to the next one and eventually Trevor's table.

Audra left before lunch, which for Alison was slightly disappointing leftovers. The casserole wasn't quite as good reheated. Between the mushy food and frustrating questions and good yet somehow bad workload, Alison started her afternoon on a cranky foot. Her mom was helping a customer when she heard the door open. Alison glanced up to keep tabs on whether or not the new arrival might want assistance. It was Trevor.

Alison knew she was partially hidden by furniture. She saw him between two bookshelves and through the slats of a chair. Yet somehow his eyes locked on hers after barely a step inside as though he knew exactly where to look. After all the times he'd snuck up on her, he probably did. He walked purposefully towards her.

Her ponytail had slipped forward over her shoulder while she was working. Alison pushed it back, then pulled it forward again. She rubbed her hands on the sides of her worn and stained jeans. This was how Trevor had seen her the other times, but she wished she could at least know if there were any smudges on her face. She smiled like someone who didn't care about smudges. "Good morning, Trevor. I saw you coming today." She hoped he understood the reference to her being startled. If he knew she'd thought of holding his table hostage, which she wasn't actually doing, it'd probably sound different.

He smiled back. "Good morning. I... it's not morning, is it?"

Alison laughed at the mistake. She'd made it first, but he looked as though she'd been trying to trip him up on purpose.

"So, yeah, I think this is the first time I didn't have to talk to that other woman first," he said. "That's how I came straight back."

Her eyes floated to her mom, who managed to squeeze in a wink while describing some options to a customer. For a guy who had assumed Alison knew his family connections, he seemed pretty oblivious to hers.

Trevor stepped closer and leaned forward. "I swear I could feel her eyes following me though. She must drive away customers with the scrutiny, but I suppose she's the boss so you can't just tell her to try to be normal."

There was sympathy in his expression now rather than amusement, which meant the joke had gone too far. He might as well have said, "Now what did you want to tell me?" Alison made sure she smiled when she said, "She's my mom."

Trevor laughed, and he was already talking before she realized that was because he thought she was kidding. "Wow. That'd be awful."

Alison found herself fighting a laugh at the misunderstanding. She didn't think she'd be able to convince him she wasn't joking while laughing so she shoved the topic aside for the moment. "Audra was disappointed not to sell any paintings this morning."

"None?" Trevor turned to the wall of art and back. "She said someone was planning to get one today."

"The woman practically begged me to hold it for her." Alison gestured to the reserved sign that Audra had wanted to keep up another week and then shrugged. "But we didn't see her. There's been so much interest in general though, I'm sure it's only a matter of time. Especially since she's practically giving them away."

He nodded, slowly. His eyes darted around as though the topic made him uncomfortable.

Now that Alison knew he'd only been teasing, she was kind of uncomfortable to remember how she'd all but yelled at him for not gushing over the paintings.

"What are you working on today?" Trevor asked, waving his hand towards the chair she'd been working on when he came in. He immediately added, "I mean, I can see it's a chair. What are you doing to improve it?"

Alison smiled. It was only funny that he asked what a chair was after he clarified that he wasn't asking what it was. She'd known what he meant. "You caught me between steps," she said. She'd been cleaning up when she spotted him. "I need to let the stain dry before I put the stupid new fabric on cushions."

"Is that a frustrating step or… Why did you call it stupid?"

Trevor seemed curious while Alison was mildly horrified. She always kept her opinions of the furniture – and particularly customers' choices regarding it – from everyone but her parents. Why was she being so unguarded with this guy? She glanced around to make sure no one was in earshot before she opened up further. "It isn't… I meant the fabric, but it really isn't. They're putting the rocker in a baby's room and picked out a slightly cartoony Noah's ark print that's actually very cute. But we've had this chair for a while, and I always thought it was kind of… stately. I thought it would end up in a formal sitting room or the lobby of a hotel or… I don't know. Someplace with a chandelier."

"Now you feel like you're ruining it with a cartoon?" he asked.

"Not ruining it. Just…" Alison paused to decide how to explain it. "I'm just not excited about changing my plan for it."

"Do you have plans for all of this?" He swept his arm towards the packed shop.

"No. It's not even something I do intentionally. Sometimes someone asks for something that feels somehow wrong, and that's when I realize I would have picked something else."

"I guess it's good I told you what I wanted before you saw my table," Trevor said. "You didn't have time to... unless you still... What do you think of my plan?"

"It's good," she said. She answered fast enough that it sounded a bit like a reflex. She was trying not to gush because she loved the way the design was unique yet subtle.

Trevor frowned. He seemed to think she was hiding more negative feelings with her pat response.

"Actually, I could bring your table out to work on next if you want to watch."

"That would be awesome!" He smiled broadly at the invitation, possibly because it was an invitation.

"You can grab one of those chairs from around that table to sit while I get it," Alison said, already moving towards the back door and away from one of the worst ideas she'd ever had.

Trevor moved towards where she pointed, and she turned around and hurried through the door. She stood on the other side of it mentally berating herself. What had possessed her to suggest such a thing? She hated to have anyone watch her work. She'd just been thinking about how many things she was supposed to finish before she started his table. The other customers wouldn't know that something had been bumped ahead, and she could sort of justify restoring someone's existing piece before getting to something new, but she still hated to have anyone watch her work.

"You need something, honey?" Alison's dad looked up from the floor where he was wrestling an unrecognizable configuration of wood.

It momentarily distracted her. "What are you doing?"

"I... uh... I need to rig up something to support a rickety pedestal, but the wood is not cooperating." He grunted as he dropped it, then shoved himself to standing and stomped one foot against the floor, possibly to return some feeling. "Need me to help you take something out?" he asked.

Alison smiled at his guess. He knew about how long the rocker would take and when she'd be ready for a new project. "I think I'll work on that one next," she said.

He pointed where she pointed. "That one?"

"Yeah. I think so."

Confusion squinted her dad's eyes and tilted his head. "You... gonna sand it by hand?"

Alison never used the loud tools in the showroom. That was another reason suggesting Trevor could watch was a monumentally bad idea. "Uh... sure," she said. "He's not changing the color so I might not need to take off too much."

Her dad shrugged and moved into position to pick up one end for her.

Alison didn't immediately reach for her side. A very brief internal battle raged instead. If her dad helped her carry the table, he would see Trevor and know exactly why she wanted to skip ahead and make more work for herself. If she insisted on carrying it alone, she would look awkward getting it through the door and might have to drag it, which would not be good for the table. Trevor might rush to help. She didn't know if that would be nice or embarrassing.

She chose to cling to a shred of normalcy and move the table with her dad's help as she would have if Trevor was not involved. It was also unlikely her dad would have allowed her to move it alone anyway. He couldn't stand by when he could be useful.

"Okay. Thanks." Alison backed through the door first. It was wide enough and the table small enough that they didn't have to do any crazy maneuvering to get through. She watched her dad's eyes widen, then narrow with a frown as he noticed the reason she wanted this table out front. Fortunately, he stayed quiet. He said nothing even when Trevor greeted him as he set the table down. He simply acknowledged the younger man with a nod and returned to his back room sanctuary.

Alison decided that the best way to deal with her lapse in judgment was to pretend it didn't happen. She would pretend Trevor wasn't watching her, that he was simply a customer taking a long time to decide whether or not that chair was comfortable. She went to her tool bench in the corner and grabbed a sanding block.

Her plan didn't improve the situation because the idea that Trevor was sitting there trying out the chair caused some giggles to bubble beneath the surface. She turned her back to him as she ran the block over the surface. Maybe he would realize that watching her work was incredibly boring and leave. Maybe she wouldn't be disappointed if he did.

It quickly became apparent that he was not bored. He asked questions about her work, some of which she struggled to answer without giving away that she had rearranged her afternoon to try to keep him around. But when the conversation moved beyond the current project to her work in general, she began to relax. She forgot to regret the impulsive invitation.

"My dad and I make a pretty good team," she said, "because he likes to fix the functionality. He gets satisfaction from making a drawer slide in and out smoothly again or steadying a wobble. He's taught me to do a lot of those things, but what I really enjoy is making something pretty."

"So do you guys tag team a lot of the furniture?" Trevor asked. "He fixes what's broken and you polish it up?"

"Sometimes." She considered the division of labor. "But sometimes there's just more fixing to do or more polishing. I don't think we directly hand things off very often because we don't want to be waiting for each other, and things don't always take as long as you think they'll take." She smiled to herself as machine noises fired up in the back room. "Case in point," she said with a nod that direction.

Trevor tipped his head in a confused bid for explanation.

"That's the table saw," Alison said. "I can tell by the sound that he's not cutting anything. He turns it on to cover the sound of him yelling at a project."

Trevor laughed with her. "I need one of those at work for when I want to mutter about something."

"Or some*one*," Alison suggested.

He nodded and sent his eyes to where Alison's mom was chatting with a customer.

Alison smiled only faintly. It was past time to end that miscommunication. "She really is my mom."

"Right," Trevor said with a chuckle and no indication that he believed it wasn't a joke. "Do you ever... When your dad does part of a project, do you wish you could have seen it through yourself from beginning to end?"

"Well, plenty of the pieces only need the cosmetic stuff." She tapped her finger on the table in front of her as an example. "So I have lots of opportunities to complete something myself, but it isn't... it doesn't bother me if I haven't done all the work as long as I have something to work on."

"You like to be busy?"

Alison nodded, then she noticed how her hand had stilled while they talked. She scrubbed harder on the tabletop. It was a beautiful piece of wood. "Did you say you used this table when you were a kid?"

"Yeah. It was at my grandparents' house, in an extra bedroom they called the playroom." Trevor seemed to be thinking quickly for more to say, as though her interest was too valuable to let pass.

Alison felt her stomach quiver at the idea that her attention mattered so much.

"All the grandkids would play in there, and I was one of the older ones so we'd keep our stuff on the table to keep the little ones from messing it up."

"Like a crawling Godzilla?"

"Exactly." Trevor smiled and caused another round of stomach quivers farther north.

Alison tried not to be concerned about her internal organs apparently migrating. A few more people had entered the shop, and her mom was engaged with one. She would need to extricate every part of her if another customer needed help.

"Grandma May put the table there initially because Ryan and I wanted to use something with small pieces with a baby around. She said we had to keep it all up high so no one would choke," Trevor said. "And once we had things out the baby's reach, it seemed like a good idea no matter how big the pieces were."

"And which of the games involved beating on this nice table?" She hoped he could tell it was only a playful reproach. "This has seen some abuse."

Trevor held his hands up in a show of innocence. "I mentioned the cousins, right? It was one of them."

Alison enjoyed the banter, but she could tell Trevor was already shifting to a more serious question.

"Does it really bother you?"

"Does what bother me?"

"Seeing nice furniture that's all damaged and dented."

"Well, that depends." Alison thought of a few pieces that had annoyed her and tried to speak in a general sense. "Sometimes I see things that are gouged in some areas and smooth in others or clearly aren't that old but still... If it looks like something's been misused or treated carelessly, that can bug me. But when I'm working on something with, like, an even coat of dents and scratches over a lifetime of use... It's hard to describe, but I almost feel like I'm part of something important when I prepare it for an extended life."

Trevor was looking at her intently when she glanced up. There was a flush of embarrassment until she read the understanding in his eyes.

"That makes sense," he said. "Working on something that's been appreciated for a long time might make your efforts seem more appreciated somehow. I think."

Alison nodded at the sentiment, feeling a small connection between them to know that she would now be tied to this table that already held a lot of memories for Trevor. The moment was interrupted by a customer in her peripheral vision who seemed to be looking around for help. She left the sander on the table as she said, "Excuse me. I need to pretend I work here."

"I'll wait," Trevor said.

The words shocked her because she realized she had expected him to wait before he said it. How had she been so presumptive? Just because she was enjoying the company didn't mean he had the time or even wanted to have the time to sit around watching her work. She shook off those thoughts to answer some questions.

A man was looking for a dresser for his daughter's room. He found one he liked and sent a picture to his wife for approval. She called him and stayed on the phone while he discussed paint and drawer pulls with Alison. A sale was great, but knowing Trevor was waiting made it seem to take forever to record all the details.

Alison thanked the man and remained facing the front as he turned for the door, not wanting to give the impression she'd been anxious for him to leave. A middle-aged couple had been browsing while she helped the customer. They left just before he did, but she'd heard them agreeing that there was too much to look at in one visit. She hoped they'd be back.

The shop was quiet now. Too quiet. Alison's mom wasn't helping anyone either. She was standing in the back next to Trevor. It sort of looked as though the two of them were having a staring contest.

Trevor said something Alison couldn't make out as she approached. He had his back to her now since he was facing the table while she worked. The low rumble of his voice made Alison's mom smile and look her way. "She's coming to rescue you now," she said.

Trevor looked over his shoulder as Alison joined them. His eyes got a little happier, not as though he was relieved at being rescued but just happy. Alison felt a hint of gooiness.

Her mom rapped on the table and said, "Nice job," before she moved towards the front of the shop.

Alison suspected she meant nice job using the table to get him to stick around, not nice job on sanding it the hard way. She only smiled in response as she returned to working on it. "I hope that didn't take too long," she said to Trevor.

Trevor waited until Alison looked up before he mouthed the words, "Is she gone?"

She nodded, wondering what creepy thing her mom had done now. The woman had been way too amused by the impression she'd given. "What did she say?"

"Not a lot really." He glanced over his shoulder to confirm for himself that they were alone. "She just kept... expecting *me* to say something, but I didn't know what."

"What do you mean?"

"Well, she came over here and said, 'So...' Then just stood there like I was supposed to fill in the blank."

"Huh."

"She asked if I came to check on the table and kept looking at me expectantly after I said yes. It was a yes or no question." He shrugged helplessly. "I eventually said you'd just started but had already made good progress. She kept waiting for more."

Alison found herself fighting a laugh. She pictured a conversation with her mom later where she explained that she'd been waiting for Trevor to admit some unexplainable feeling that made him come in to check on the table.

"I'm not getting you in trouble by being here while you're working, am I?" he asked.

"No." She dismissed the idea with a wave of her hand.

"Are you sure? Because..." Trevor trailed off sounding genuinely concerned.

"I'm sure." Alison sat on the floor and slid a finger down one of the bare table legs. She'd gotten the whole thing pretty smooth and was only delaying starting another step. "I'm here the whole sixty hours a week we're open. But that's a long week. I'm not actively working the whole time. Now and then we'll even set up a game on one of the tables and just pause it when someone comes in."

"You and..." He tipped his head towards the front to indicate her mom.

Alison nodded. "Sometimes my dad plays, too."

"Right." Trevor's eyes snapped to the wide door as though maybe he'd forgotten someone was back there occasionally making a lot of noise. "Have either of you ever wondered..."

"Wondered what?" she prompted. She leaned closer for encouragement. He seemed to be hesitating about whatever he wanted to ask.

He glanced around and lowered his voice. "That woman asked whose idea it was for me to watch you work, and when I said yours, she cracked up like that was hilarious. Have you ever wondered if she might be... a little... unhinged?"

Now Alison hesitated. She needed to defend her mom, but she didn't want to explain how she thought it was funny that her daughter had done something way out of character for a guy she'd been trying to insist she didn't think much about.

"Alison!" Her dad's voice called to her from where his head was poking out of the back room. "Who's making dinner tonight? I have a hankering for something off the grill."

"I think it's Mom's turn," she said.

He peeked around to see if there were any customers – other than Trevor, who apparently didn't count – before he yelled louder. "Elaine! What are you making for dinner?"

She began to walk towards the back as she answered him. "I haven't decided yet."

"Do you mind if I fire up the grill?"

"If you're volunteering to cook, you can make whatever you want."

"Maybe you could cut up some lettuce and tomato to go with some burgers."

"Do we have any tomatoes left?" Her voice got quieter as she reached the door and was reduced to mumbled noise as she joined him on the other side of it.

Alison wondered why her parents were talking about dinner already. Then she checked the big clock on the wall. Her eyes bugged out. It was nearly 5:30. It had been barely 2 o'clock when Trevor came in. How had they been talking so long? What had they even been talking about?

He must have noticed the time as well because he was already putting his chair back. "I've, uh, probably been here long enough and... I'll let you work in peace or... yeah." He sort of pointed at the table and waved at the same time.

Alison took that to mean he would be in touch or expect a call when it was ready. She waved back after he'd already turned away. It was a strange goodbye, but she felt certain it was not a final one so she only puzzled over it for a few moments.

12

hy did the sun have to be so bright in the morning? If Trevor was honest with himself, he'd have to admit it was a tad easier to get out of bed when the sun did it first. But it was hard to be grateful when it was blinding him. There was something about the angle this time of year that felt as though the rays were attacking him when he entered the January Café. Maybe he needed to tell his grandma not to polish the door, not that she'd follow that advice.

She almost seemed to be laughing at it as he heard her higher laugh mixed in with all the male voices. What could possibly be so funny this early? Trevor heard some greetings as the laughter died. He nodded that direction, still squinting. The shape of Grandma May floated out of the crowd and reached the back of the counter as he reached the front.

"Look what the cat dragged in," she said. "It's my favorite grandchild."

"Good morning, Grandma May," he mumbled.

"Same to you." She grinned cheerfully. "Now say please."

"Huh?"

"I know you'd like a cup of coffee, but it wouldn't hurt you to make a polite request."

Trevor wasn't convinced it wouldn't hurt. "May I please have a cup of your fine coffee?" he said, because he was just awake enough to know he'd be scolded if he dared to suggest it was too early to be polite.

She nabbed a mug from under the counter and placed it in front of him before she disappeared into the kitchen for coffee to put in it. She added a small spoon of sugar without making him be polite again.

"Thank you," he said, pulling the drink close. People talked about running on fumes as though it was a bad thing, but Trevor wondered if the scent didn't wake him up as well as the caffeine. He leaned forward to inhale deeply.

"Matt's leaving us."

Trevor blinked at the abrupt statement. Matt was the manager of the restaurant. If by leaving she meant quitting, this was big and shocking news. "When?" he asked.

"Not immediately, but..." She sighed and backed up to the beginning of the explanation. "His mother-in-law is... her health is failing. His wife wants to move closer to be able to help. Of course, I fully support a man putting his family before his job so we'll have to let him go without a fuss. It'll be some time to get their house on the market and pack up and everything so we'll probably have a month to find a replacement."

"I'm sorry to hear that," Trevor said. "I mean, about his wife and her mom."

Grandma May acknowledged the sentiment with a quick nod. She paused to let Trevor sip his coffee. "Matt's been running this place for nearly ten years," she observed.

He was catching up to that thought. He knew his grandparents had always trusted Matt and that Trevor had only ever heard good things about him. The man would be difficult to replace. Unfortunately, Trevor didn't think he could do anything to help.

"Grandpa Paul and I have been thinking it over. We'd like to ask Ryan if he'd be interested in the job." She spoke slowly, softly, letting her words drift towards him through the morning fog. "But we wanted to make sure there would be no hard feelings from the rest of you. What do you think?"

He thought that people shouldn't ask him serious questions when they had to speak slowly to do it. He breathed in some of that flavorful steam as he considered. It made sense that they thought of Ryan. He needed a good job. He'd gotten one he liked right after college. That company went out of business a few years later, and he'd had a couple he liked a lot less since. He'd moved in with Trevor about six months ago to save on rent while he contemplated another job change, possibly even a return to school.

But would he enjoy managing the restaurant? Had he ever thought about it? Those were questions for Ryan. Why was Grandma May looking at Trevor for an answer? Something about hard feelings? He took a sip of wake-up juice.

"We wouldn't necessarily give it to him," she said. "But we won't be around forever and…we could talk about silent partners or something. No one's getting rich here though."

Oh. Trevor had never really thought about what might happen to the restaurant when his grandparents decided to retire for real. Now that he started thinking about it, he liked the idea of keeping it in the family. Would he be envious if it belonged to his brother? It was a restaurant. Trevor wasn't much of a cook. Most of their employees were high school or college students who didn't last long. He would not enjoy constantly training new people or looking for those new people. Plus, there was the fact that the place opened at 6 AM.

Trevor set down the mug to share his new insights. "You should ask Ryan," he said. "I like the idea of keeping the place in the family, but I don't want it."

Grandma May sighed. "You're very blunt in the morning."

He realized he'd offended her by saying he didn't want something she'd spent much of her life pouring her heart into.

"That's okay," she said, recovering before he could apologize. "I know you meant to say you don't think you could run it as well as we have."

Trevor nodded. If it made her feel better, that was exactly what he meant to say.

"Besides…" Her bright smile returned. "I know you're more interested in the business next door."

"Nope." Trevor hated to ruin her smile again, but she needed to know that her expectations were way off. "That's over, over before it started."

She looked confused but no less hopeful. "Now how can that be? I heard you spent several hours with her on Saturday."

It was Trevor's turn to be confused. How had she heard that? Saturday was only two days ago, and he hadn't told anyone. He didn't think he'd told anyone. His memory was still sluggish. He was pretty sure he'd been keeping the disaster close to the vest.

Grandma May leaned against her side of the counter with concern in her eyes. "Didn't you have a nice time talking with Alison?"

Of course he had, but she was never going to speak to him again. Except that he had to collect his table at some point. He'd really made a terrific mess.

"You like her. I can tell you do, so what's the problem?" Her question was unusually pushy given that she hadn't asked about Alison at all before. She simply brought up related topics and counted on Trevor being too groggy to stop himself from letting things slip.

"The problem is… I didn't know she was her mom."

Grandma May stepped back with her hands on her hips as though his idiocy was so big she needed more room to take it all in. That was Trevor's impression anyway. More likely, she was just confused by an answer that left out a lot of details. "How is that a problem?"

"I definitely wouldn't have said what I said if I'd known," he said.

"Did you… insult Elaine somehow?"

For a moment, Trevor shifted his focus from Alison onto making sure his grandma didn't think he was a monster. "Not on purpose and not to her face." The moment was over. "Alison was horrified, and rightfully so. I blew it."

"Well, now… if it wasn't on purpose, I'm sure it's entirely forgivable." Grandma May leaned against the counter again. "You could go over there right now to –"

"No," Trevor said. "It's over. I was already on about my fifth chance. It's over."

Instead of the sympathy he expected, she looked at him as though she was greatly disappointed. Well, he was disappointed in himself. He tried to enjoy some coffee – it didn't work – while Grandpa Paul called her attention to his corner table.

"Hey, May. We need you to settle something."

"Settle what?" She called back from where she was without bothering to move closer to the conversation.

"Have we always had the smokey links on the menu?" he asked.

She shook her head. "No. We only served patties up until three or four years ago."

"Really!?" Grandpa Paul sounded disbelieving. Several of the other guys were laughing and pointing at him. It appeared she had not settled the debate in his favor.

Trevor shared a smile with his grandmother over the reaction. It was a great opportunity to move on from his failure, but Alison was sticking in his head. "I don't suppose I could just happen to stop by your house for a visit when she delivers the table so she doesn't have to force herself to be polite." It was a lame joke.

"The table." Grandma May exhaled the words as though she was relieved to be reminded of it.

"What about the table?"

She didn't answer, and she was staring into space.

Trevor had a few sips of coffee while he waited for her mind to return to him. He needed to drink faster because his time was getting short.

Her eyes traveled back to his and seemed to study him without really seeing him. "I wonder if it's time to bring in reinforcements," she said.

"You lost me, Grandma."

She continued to stare, then blinked as she came back. "You'll keep our conversation about Ryan to yourself until Grandpa and I have a chance to talk to him?"

"Of course," he said. She didn't need to ask. She knew that, too, which made him think she was trying to change the subject. "Are you going to tell me what you were just talking about?"

"Hmm?" She squinted her eyes to match the confused noise.

"Reinforcements and all that?"

"Oh. I was just thinking out loud."

"Why do I feel like it's something I should know?"

She smiled indulgently, like he was a little boy asking for an extra helping of dessert. "You let your older and wiser grandmother worry about what you should know."

"I suppose you're entitled to be a little eccentric from time to time."

"I think he's finally awake and talking sense." She winked at Trevor.

"May, are you sure about those sausages?" Grandpa Paul called.

"Yes, I'm sure." She said it loudly but without even looking his direction.

Trevor downed the last of his coffee. "I better go."

"Already?" She checked her watch. "Oh, you were kind of late this morning."

"Sorry we didn't have more time to chat."

She smiled. "As long as you're coming back tomorrow?"

He pushed himself from the chair as he assured her it was his favorite part of the day.

She gladly accepted the only partially facetious compliment.

13

"Tell me again why we're playing on the floor?"

Trevor narrowed his eyes at Ryan, who wasn't really expecting an answer. He was only complaining. "Because we don't have a table right now."

"You didn't have a table last week," Logan said, "and we met at Audra's."

"Did she kick us out or something?" Cameron asked. He sounded as though he thought it unlikely.

Ryan looked at Trevor, who was the one who'd turned down the offer to use her place again.

"We don't need Audra looking over everyone's shoulders," Trevor said.

"You know she'll be here anyway," Ryan pointed out.

"Just deal," Trevor said.

Ryan held out his hand to Logan for the cards. Logan checked to verify it was Ryan's turn before he passed them.

The truth was that Trevor had known that playing at his sister's place would be a constant reminder of his missing table. He'd failed to appreciate that sitting on the floor would be just as constant and significantly more uncomfortable as well. Then he'd gotten that text. There was no way he wasn't thinking about Alison, but at least this way Audra wasn't trying to talk to him about her.

The door flew open as Audra stepped inside. "Hello, guys," she said. "Oops." She turned around and held on to the door as she reached outside to ring the doorbell before she closed it behind her.

"Very funny," Trevor said dryly.

"You can stop pretending that you're not leaving the door open for me," she said. "And why are you playing on the floor?"

Trevor sighed. "We just had this conversation."

"I'm not sure anyone actually answered the question," Cameron said.

"I thought you must have found, like, a folding table or something," Audra said.

Logan looked up at her. "Can we move to your place after this hand?"

"Sure." She smiled. "I think Violet was missing you guys."

"She'd be welcome to wander over here with you," Ryan said.

Audra snorted. "Probably more welcome than I am." She was clearly referring to all the cards being held out of her view. She stepped around behind Logan, and Trevor lowered his eyes before he caught a wince or a smile.

It likely would have been a smile because Logan stood up as soon as he played his last card, and it didn't take long. He seemed more interested in talking to Audra than stretching his legs, but it made the other guys more eager to get to their feet.

Trevor was the last to stand and the last out the door. He wasn't trying to drag his feet. He was only preoccupied. As amazing as Alison was, she wasn't amazing for his Tichu game. It'd be shocking that he and Ryan were winning if they were more than three hands in.

Audra entered first and yelled, "I'm back, and I'm not alone," as she opened her door.

By the time Trevor had closed it and paused at the new painting sitting out to dry – even Audra's work was going to remind him of Alison now that so much of it was on display at her store –

and approached the table, the other three guys had taken their seats. Audra and Violet were both standing behind Logan. Well, Violet was standing behind Audra, who was standing behind Logan.

"You ladies might as well have a seat if you're going to watch," Ryan said. Their table was larger. It had six chairs around it. He nodded to the one next to him.

Audra didn't need a second invitation. She pulled the chair out and towards the corner so she could see around to Logan's hand. He was shuffling and didn't have one yet, but she was ready.

Violet looked uncertainly at the other empty chair next to Trevor. He nodded at her. She smiled at the permission and moved to claim the seat. He hoped he hadn't implied permission to watch his cards. An audience was a worse idea than usual when he knew he was likely to misplay the hand. But he and his friends were invading her space so he'd make the concession if necessary.

Audra picked up Logan's cards as he dealt them. He scowled at her. She smiled very sweetly back so he said nothing. After she'd looked at the first eight and shook her head at Logan – not a complete giveaway of his hand – she put the cards back down and eyed Trevor. "I talked to Grandma today."

There was something very familiar about the teasing way she said it. Trevor responded with some curiosity though. This couldn't be about Alison. He'd been firm in avoiding details all week so all his grandma knew was that the situation was hopeless. Audra could be annoying, but she wasn't heartless enough to tease him about that. It didn't appear she was going to tease him about anything. She was looking back at him as though he was the one with something to say.

"And?" he finally said.

"She had a good idea." Again she seemed to be waiting for him to run with the thought.

"And that idea was what?" Logan asked.

Audra only smiled wider, happy to be making everyone curious. Trevor involuntarily followed her eyes as they danced around the table. When they flit over Ryan, he made a guess about what she was almost bringing up. Grandma May had said Audra was fully on board, but she hadn't mentioned whether or not she'd had a chance to discuss it with Ryan. "I don't know if we're supposed to talk about this yet," Trevor said.

"Talk about what?" Audra said. She was somewhat distracted watching Logan fan out his cards.

"You tell me," Trevor said. "You're the one who brought up Grandma and her ideas." He sent a pointed glance at Ryan. Audra missed it because she was pointing out something to Logan that he probably didn't need pointed out.

"If either of you are talking about Grandma asking me to take over for Matt," Ryan said, "she and Grandpa asked me about it yesterday."

"You're going to work at the café?" Violet asked him.

"Maybe."

"Do you want the job?" Trevor asked.

Audra asked what he had told their grandparents at the same time. Cameron and Logan pushed their cards together to show that a potential job change deserved full attention.

Ryan glanced around at all the pairs of eyes on him. "I think I'm excited about it, but I never considered it before so I asked if I could have a few days to think about it. They actually arranged for me to shadow Matt on Monday so I'll have a better idea what it is I'm thinking about."

"Cool," Logan said. "I guess you're going to call in sick to your regular job that day."

Ryan pretended to cough, which earned a few smiles. Then he fanned his cards out along with the others.

It was something of a relief to Trevor that he still had no hard feelings as he heard Ryan leaning towards taking the job. It wasn't something he'd considered before his grandma put him on the spot. And it had been early then so he might not have fully appreciated his own mind. He did appreciate the impressive hand he'd been dealt. The round went well for him and Ryan. And quickly.

As Logan began to collect the cards, Audra said, "Okay, now we can talk about what I was really trying to talk about."

"What did you want to talk about?" Logan asked.

"Something more important?" Ryan raised an eyebrow daring her to agree.

"Of course not," she said. "A new job is very important, but I didn't know if you'd want to talk about it yet since Grandma told me you were still thinking about it." Audra turned to Trevor without taking a breath. "I saw you at church on Sunday."

He almost laughed at what seemed a very random comment. "I know," he said. "I saw you, too. You came up and asked me what I was doing there. Not very welcoming."

She ignored the last comment, as it was intended. "You told me that you'd gotten busy on Saturday and lost track of time."

Trevor nodded even though he now knew where her leading tone was leading.

"Grandma told me that you lost track of time," pause for air quotes, "at Next Love with Alison."

"Really?" A look of understanding crossed Ryan's face. "Had a plan, huh?"

"It wasn't a plan," Trevor said. "I just thought I'd check on the table in person."

"And that took *hours*?" Audra said doubtfully.

Violet made some sort of squealing noise.

"Hours?" Logan nodded approvingly. "That sounds promising."

"Yeah, it was." Trevor took a moment to remember when it had seemed promising, when he had hopes of Alison agreeing to go out. She had invited him to stay, after all, which seemed like proof she wasn't repulsed by his company. And they'd had a great time just talking. He tried and failed to pause the memory before things turned awful. He had no intention of sharing that part, and the guys seemed fine with the conversation ending right there.

Audra, however, appeared far less satisfied. "You see why I'm confused, right?"

It sounded like a rhetorical question. Trevor took the cards from Logan, cut them, and began to deal.

"I'll bite," Logan said. "Why are you confused? Something to do with your brother having an intelligent conversation that long?"

There were a few smiles at the jab. Audra was shaking her head though. "No. I'm confused because a long talk, where people aren't paying attention to the time, that sounds great. Promising, as someone here said. But Grandma said you were giving up. Why?"

"It's really none of your business."

"It sort of is," Audra said. She actually seemed to believe that.

"What?"

"Well, I'm going to see Alison tomorrow. If she might kick my paintings off the wall because you offended her, it'll be easier to talk her out of it if I know what happened."

Trevor rolled his eyes. "She wouldn't do that."

"I don't think you even want to be in business with someone who'd be petty enough to hold you responsible for something someone else did," Ryan added.

Trevor nodded because it was good to have someone on his side.

"Was it something you did or something you said?" Ryan asked, smiling at Audra and effectively switching sides.

"I would like to know," Audra said. "What if I unknowingly rub salt in the wound or something?"

"You'll be fine," Trevor said.

Audra sighed and leaned over to peek at the cards Logan had just picked up. She only studied them a few moments before she looked back at Trevor. "Grandma said it had something to do with her mom?"

"Whose mom?" Violet asked.

"Alison's."

"Her mom doesn't approve of you or something?" Now Violet looked confused.

Trevor felt small comfort in the idea that not approving of him was confusing, though still preferred the topic be dropped. It seemed the only hope he could play Tichu in peace was to go ahead and admit how dumb he was. "Fine, I'll tell you," he said. "I asked Alison if she was worried her mom might be insane."

Now there were a lot of confused eyes on him.

"You mean, like, a joke?" Audra asked.

"No. I asked her seriously, as if she might have concerns for her safety with the woman around because I didn't know she was her mom."

"Her mom works there, too?" Logan asked.

Ryan said, "Why would she be concerned?"

"Wait a minute." Audra jumped in before Trevor could answer the questions he didn't want to answer anyway. "You never actually called her creepy around Alison, did you?"

"Oh!" Logan's eyes widened. "The creepy woman turned out to be Alison's mom?"

Trevor nodded.

Logan and Cameron winced. They seemed to understand how badly he'd screwed up. That wasn't something Trevor felt particularly good about being understood.

"Still confused," Audra said. "She seemed very nice to me. Why were you even calling her the creepy woman?"

"I wasn't. Not really, I..." Trevor felt guilty and defensive, which was an uncomfortable combination. He spilled out more words than he might have otherwise to relieve the pressure of it. "I was just sort of annoyed with mornings in general when I thought she was being creepy, and careless when it slipped out. But Alison laughed so of course I couldn't resist continuing the joke. I said something on Saturday about her being creepy, and Alison actually told me she was her mom, and I didn't believe her because I thought she was kidding. I thought she... like an inside joke between us. Her mom was being kind of obvious about spying on us, which now that I know who she is is kind of funny, but I didn't know. Something about the way she laughed at... Alison looked fairly shocked by my question. There's no way to come back from, 'I think your mom might be a dangerous lunatic.'"

The guys at the table turned to their cards as though that was the end of the story. Because it was. But Audra was like a puppy that kept coming back for more tug-of-war no matter how many times it fell on its butt when someone let go. "I still don't see how that ruins everything," she said. "I mean, if you were getting along for... hours, apparently... one comment isn't enough to... You just say, 'I'm sorry. I didn't realize she was your mom.'"

"Did you not hear the part where she already told me?" Trevor put down the cards he wanted to pass.

"Could she tell you thought she was kidding?" Violet said. "Because then you could argue that the misunderstanding was kind of her fault for not correcting you sooner." She and Audra were nodding at each other.

Trevor generally thought Violet was nice enough, but at the moment he wished he was still sitting on the floor in his apartment. He didn't need anyone backing up his sister's need to pry. "Yeah," he said, "I'll just go back and tell her it's her fault I'm an idiot."

Audra snorted at the sarcasm. "We mean she'll be more understanding of your mistake, not that you should accuse her of anything."

Trevor picked up his new cards, finally, and played a straight with the one. Now that the round had started, Audra should leave him alone. She did. For about the two minutes it took for Cameron and Logan to go out first and second with a Tichu bonus to obliterate the lead he and Ryan had. He tossed his leftover cards onto the table.

"Don't give up," Audra said.

The round was over. It took Trevor a moment to realize she was the one who still hadn't given up. "I blew it, Audra. Let it go."

She stared hard at him, thinking, probably not about letting anything go.

"He still has to get the table," Violet observed. "He could try to judge if she still seems mad then."

Audra nodded.

Trevor rolled his eyes. "I have to pay her so she can't tell me to get out even if she wants to."

"When are you going to get the table?" Cameron asked. His interest seemed to be solidly in the table. Or rather, when their weekly game could go back to normal.

"Hopefully by next Friday," Trevor said. "It's ready, but I haven't scheduled the delivery." That's why Alison had texted him that afternoon, to let him know it was finished. She asked if he wanted to set up a delivery time or come to the store to inspect it first. Trevor wanted to stop in first because then he could see her twice whereas if she delivered it right away, that would be the last time. She could even send her dad, which would be easier for her. Unless he found something wrong. Then it would just be one more way he'd wasted her time. Of course he didn't have to say anything. He could live with, say, two of the suits with their colors reversed as a permanent monument to his failure. That thought was so dramatic he'd stepped back to ask himself what he'd do if a beautiful, wonderful woman wasn't involved. He'd want to see it first.

"When will you?" Audra asked.

"When will I... have it delivered?"

"When will you schedule the delivery?" She sighed as though that had been obvious.

"I guess some time tomorrow," Trevor said.

Audra nodded. But she seemed suspiciously thoughtful, as though she was dropping the subject for the night but not forever.

14

She looked very sunny as she walked in wearing a blouse with ruffles and little yellow flowers. Alison decided not to say anything about the guy who'd been in the previous day asking when the artist would be available to sell him a painting. She wasn't going to get Audra's hopes up a third week in a row.

Audra waved at Alison's mom as she passed. As usual, she was talking to a customer. Sometimes it seemed she spent a lot more time talking to customers than selling them anything. Audra walked right up to Alison and smiled in a strange, knowing way. Then the expression disappeared as she pulled a sketchbook out from under her arm.

"I brought some paper today," she said. "I thought I could doodle some ideas if or *when* I have some downtime. But it's probably a terrible idea." She let her arm flop to the side with the book. "When I try to sketch out painting ideas, I always end up staring at a blank page while I sort of paint in my head."

Alison nodded. She didn't consider herself as much of an artist, but she thought she still understood. She sometimes tried to draw things before she got them on the furniture. That was mostly about planning the scale and measurements. A pencil and a paintbrush were very different tools.

"Maybe I'll make a shopping list," Audra said with a shrug. Then she pointed behind Alison. "Hey! Is that Trevor's table?"

"Yeah." Alison moved closer to it with Audra.

"It looks awesome!" Audra said. "I'm not sure I'd even recognize it if I didn't know he asked for the suits along the edge. That was my idea. Sort of. Okay, not really. I suggested he have you do a giant sword across the middle." She waved her hand over the area without actually touching it. "I think this... Don't tell him I said so, but he might have been right about it being too much. This is perfect. It's like a brand-new table."

If Trevor was half as excited about Alison's work as his sister, she was going to feel pretty good. Actually, she already felt pretty good hearing Audra's praise.

"Can I touch it?" she asked. "I mean, it's not wet or anything?"

"Go ahead."

Audra lightly ran a finger over the four symbols on the edge closest to her before she looked up again. "I don't suppose you know how to play Tichu."

She shook her head. She'd gotten sidetracked while studying the symbols and read the rules. The game sounded fun. And complicated. It wouldn't be fair to say she knew how to play until she'd tried.

"I miss it." Audra sounded wistful. "I used to play with my brothers. We all learned together... me and Trevor and Ryan and Logan. We played a lot. Then maybe a little over a year ago, they invited Cameron to play, turned it into a guy thing. I don't think they really meant to kick me out, but..." She forced herself to brighten. "I taught Violet how to play though and if I taught you, we'd only need one more to have our own girls' Tichu nights."

"That could be fun," Alison said. She honestly liked the idea. Audra was quickly beginning to feel like a real friend. And now that she was beginning to think a relationship with Trevor was a possibility, getting better acquainted with his family would be a plus. Alison thought about asking if inviting her mom to be the fourth might be okay.

Audra spoke up first. "We can't ask my mom. I love her and all, but she's kind of hopeless at Tichu. She keeps notes next to her and still plays the wrong thing all the time. My dad is better. He used to be our substitute when Logan couldn't come over or when Ryan was at school, but of course that would defeat the idea of it being a girl thing."

They both turned towards the front as the door opened. Audra mostly looked that way because Alison did. The customer was familiar.

"I think..." Alison said. "I might be wrong, but I think that guy was in here yesterday asking about your art."

Audra sucked in a breath as she smiled. Then she waved a hand over her face and tried to appear calm. Her eyes were still sparkly though. The guy was definitely heading towards them.

"Hello again." He held up a hand and waved with some distance still between them. "Alison, right?"

"That's right," she said with a nod.

"Will I be able to meet the artist today?" His eyes darted hopefully to Audra. He was a man of maybe sixty or sixty-five with a decent amount of pepper remaining in his hair. He was short and stocky but with a large presence.

"Yes, sir," Alison said. "This is Audra Norman. She's the one who painted all the wonderful pictures here."

"George Gomez," he said. He held out a hand to Audra as he took the last step between them.

She nodded and could only get out a hello before he continued.

"I was talking to Alison yesterday about how much I liked your work and would love a chance to talk to you about it. Can we start with the snowy one?" He was already moving towards the painting he meant.

Alison tried to wish Audra luck with a smile when she glanced back. Then she turned to her work area. There was a squat four-drawer dresser in front of her that needed handles. The customer had been fairly vague about the choice. She wanted something silver-toned, either all the same or all different. Alison had brought out the first box of handles just before Audra arrived. She sat on the floor and began to dig through the supply.

Mr. Gomez was certainly talking Audra's ear off about her work. His voice carried so that Alison could hear him even above the shifting hardware, though most of Audra's responses were lost to the noise. He asked what this was and how long that took and what type of paint did she use. He showered generous praise and told her of the things that came to mind when he gazed at the pictures.

Alison had to take a break to check on a woman who seemed interested in a table. She was told that the woman wanted to think about it and might be back. Audra was still tied up as Alison returned to her project. The man seemed very nice, but it would still be a blow if he took all this time and still didn't take a painting home. It turned out all his discussion was a way of narrowing his choices. He bought not one but two paintings and even left them for Alison's family to frame.

Audra managed to keep up a professional demeanor during the transaction. She busted into a crazy happy dance the moment the door closed behind him. A young couple came in a short time later for a set of dining chairs. They quickly picked out a painting as well. That was another frame sale. And only a few minutes before Audra planned to leave for the day, the woman who had insisted on having a painting reserved finally came in to claim it. She intended to frame it herself.

The frames were small sales, but Alison wouldn't have been disappointed anyway. It was impossible to look at Audra's exhilaration and feel anything other than a reflection of it. She was ready to go and staring at the wall, mesmerized by the four empty places.

"Part of me wants to rearrange these pictures so there aren't holes," she said. "And part of me wants to leave the holes as proof to anyone who didn't buy one that some people do like my work." She sighed, a happy sigh, as she continued. "I know that's not fair. Plenty of people can like my paintings and just not have a place to put one right now. I'm just babbling because I feel..." She bounced as she thought of a description and came up with, "Yay!"

Alison smiled. "I'm excited, too. This means you're going to bring in new pictures for me to enjoy next week, right?"

"Right." Audra's mouth fell open. She'd gotten an idea. "What about before? If I... figured out a way to get some replacements here earlier in the week, that would be okay?"

"Sure."

Audra grinned. Her eyes roved those empty places one more time. "Okay. Your mom's not busy. I need to talk to her real quick before I leave. See you next Saturday."

Alison waved and turned back to her project. The old finish had been removed and the holes filled. She had new handles picked out. It was time to start making it pretty again.

****

Alison was thinking that the furniture was prettier than she was by the afternoon. She'd left the first dresser to dry and moved on to painting another one white for a kids' room. Her ponytail had come loose, and she'd fixed it without realizing there was a glob of paint on her finger until she felt the stickiness against her hair. The drawers for both were spread over her work area so that she was constantly stepping over something and working up a sweat with all the extra movement.

She wasn't expecting Trevor at a particular time, but she slipped into the bathroom to wash her face when she thought it might be getting close. Her pulse picked up just a touch every time the front door opened. It opened too much because when Trevor did come in, she was stuck trying to explain to someone why four or five hours of custom work wasn't free.

Alison tried to keep her focus on the potential-though-unlikely customer but was still aware of Trevor walking to the back where he appeared to browse furniture near her work area. Content that he was waiting, she returned her full attention to politely answering questions on why the guy could buy the desk as is and do the work himself, but he couldn't use their space or supplies.

Alison's mom came to rescue her before she rolled her eyes or strangled him. "Hello, sir," she said. "I'm afraid Alison has a customer waiting to check on an order. I can help you while she helps him."

"Great," he said. "Can you tell me why you have to take the handles off to paint? Because it seems to me it would save time to just paint around them."

Alison nodded as she stepped away to confirm the transfer without – she hoped – looking overly grateful. She was grateful though. Her mom could have simply talked to Trevor herself. It occurred to her that it might have served a purpose though. If she had managed to finish with the other customer first, she could have walked up and addressed her as Mom, which would have finally put that issue to rest. Unlikely that she'd have finished first though.

She felt suddenly nervous as it became clear that Trevor didn't see her coming. It would only be fair if she got a turn to startle him, but she preferred a more natural greeting so she moved to the center of the shop where her approach would be obvious.

He glanced up, smiled faintly, then dropped his eyes to the chair back his fingers were skimming.

"Sorry about the wait," Alison said.

"It's no problem."

"Have you already had a chance to inspect the table?"

"Yeah, I kicked the tires." He shook his head. "I sound like my grandma."

"And what do you think?" she asked.

"Oh, I..." Trevor finally made eye contact and held it. "I think it's perfect. It's like I can tell it's the same table and yet it looks like a new one. It kind of blows my mind a little."

Alison nodded with a slight swelling of satisfaction. That was exactly as she wanted all customers to feel. Except perhaps with his mind intact. "I'm glad you approve," she said. His approval meant all they had to do was pick a day for the delivery. Alison wanted to try to get him to stay and talk for a bit first. "Did you notice that Audra sold some paintings?"

"She did?" He turned to the wall and did something of a double take. "Wait. More than one?"

"She sold four this morning," Alison said.

"Wow. Good for her." The accolade sounded genuine, but he quickly pushed it aside. "Of course, she's not going to be able to talk about anything else now."

"She *was* very excited." Alison smiled. "She kept it together in front of her customers though, happy but professional."

Trevor nodded. "So... um..." His eyes went back to the table, and Alison knew he was about to ask about a delivery time.

She threw out a quick question to stall him. "What do you do for a living?"

"Huh?"

Yeah. It had been abrupt. She waved a hand around the shop. "I just... We've spent a good amount of time talking about my job. I feel like I should know yours by now."

He shrugged. "I work at the car dealership down at the corner."

"You're a salesman!?" She sounded way more shocked than she intended. But he'd once accused her of being a salesman as though it was a bad thing.

"No." Fortunately, he seemed amused by her shock, not offended. "I keep track of inventory and sales and... It's a relatively small operation so just various record keeping and occasional research on the competition or something. Maybe an errand here and there."

"Oh." She could think of several follow-up questions she wanted to ask. She hesitated because he didn't appear all that interested in talking about it.

He tapped on the table. "I guess I need to pay you for this and then figure out when to get it back to my place."

"Okay. Follow me." She led him to the counter and efficiently completed the business part of their relationship. Then he left.

He walked out the front door as though the table had been the only reason he came in. Alison gaped after him. Had she let her mom talk her into seeing interest that wasn't there? What about last Saturday when they'd talked for hours? What about Audra saying her brother was obsessed? Was it all going to come to nothing?

Her maudlin thoughts were interrupted by laughter. Her mom was still talking to that irritating guy, yet now they were both laughing. That was weirder than that hair color she'd tried.

15

"Look what the cat dragged in. It's my favorite grandchild."

Trevor smiled. Not only was it early, it was early on a Monday morning and he'd had a lousy weekend. Yet Trevor smiled. Grandma May looked so cheerful, so sincerely happy to see him that he couldn't resist the impulse.

It was fleeting. He was probably scowling as he reached for the counter.

Grandpa Paul called out to him before he could get himself onto the high vinyl chair. "Trevor! Get over here, son."

He moved automatically towards that back table.

"I'll have a cup for you when you get back," Grandma May said.

All five old guys were looking at him as he neared their table. Fred and John and… what's-his-name and… Trevor knew all their names, but it was too early to recite them even in his head. Something in their eyes suggested they were prepared to be entertained. It did not make him look forward to the conversation. He focused on his grandpa to see what he wanted.

"You gonna say good morning?"

It wasn't. "Good morning," Trevor said anyway.

"Got a question for you," Grandpa Paul said. He paused and seemed to be waiting for an answer, but he hadn't asked the question yet.

A couple of grins popped up around the table.

"Yes?" Trevor said.

"Is that your answer?"

"To what question?"

"Don't tease the boy when he hasn't had his coffee," Grandma May hollered.

Trevor looked her way as the men laughed. There was a cup of coffee sitting on the counter in front of her, his coffee. He could have it as soon as he finished here. Why was he over here again?

"Hello!" The voice of his great aunt added to the confusion as he hadn't heard the door open. She was halfway to the counter when she saluted the back corner and said, "Top of the morning to ya, geezers."

"What kind of greeting is that?" one of them shot back.

"The one I felt like offering." She plunked a huge purse on the counter before she plunked herself onto a chair and addressed her sister in a raised voice. "Am I missing the sign that lists which greetings are allowed in here, May? Is that why I haven't heard anyone wish *me* a good morning?"

Grandma May smiled at her. "You want breakfast today?"

"Eggs would be lovely. Thanks."

"Back in a jiffy," she said, already heading towards the kitchen.

Aunt Myra glanced at the mug next to her, then at Trevor. "This yours?"

"Hang on, Trevor. I'm not done with you."

Trevor hadn't realized he'd taken a step towards the coffee until Grandpa Paul asked him to stay.

Grandpa Paul held up his left hand. "You see this knuckle on my thumb, how it doesn't straighten all the way? Tell the boys how I did that."

"Uh… you fell?"

Some of the old guys chuckled.

Grandpa groaned. "You call that a story?"

"Isn't that what happened?" Trevor taxed his sleepy brain to determine if he was mixing up details. "That's when you were running from the bees, right?"

His grandpa shook his head in disgust. "What he means is I was leading Phil from the bees he riled. I was rescuing him."

Phil was Grandpa Paul's younger brother. He'd been the one to poke the hive. Trevor nodded. That was what he said.

"Usually, it's better to have someone else tout your heroics, but this one's useless." Grandpa Paul waved a hand to dismiss Trevor back to the counter. "I'll have to tell this story myself."

Aunt Myra yelled, "I can tell them about you running from the bees."

"You weren't there," Grandpa Paul said. "I don't need your help."

Trevor took the seat next to his aunt as she muttered, "The kid wasn't there either." She was fishing around in her purse for something while he enjoyed his first drink and felt perked up by the aroma.

Grandma May returned holding a plate of scrambled eggs and toast in one hand and a coffee mug in the other. Both were white like the counter and sometimes seemed as bright as the red stripes on the chairs. Everything in the place was bright.

"How you doing this morning?" Grandma May was looking at Trevor, and Aunt Myra pushed her bag aside to listen while she ate.

"Fine," he said.

She wrinkled her nose as though the answer was barely acceptable. "How're your card club guys?"

"It's not a card club, but they're all fine."

"That coffee kicking in?" She leaned her elbows on the counter and seemed to be asking if he was awake enough to answer a real question.

Trevor was at least awake enough to recognize the shift away from small talk. He nodded and met her eyes.

"Good," she said. "I'd like you to come in for lunch today."

"Why?"

"Ryan's coming in at eleven to shadow Matt. You and Audra should be here."

"Does he need a welcoming committee?" Trevor knew he sounded a bit flippant compared to her serious tone, but he really didn't understand why she was making this request.

"You don't need to be here right at eleven," she said. "You and Audra come in at noon and have lunch while he's here."

Trevor scratched his head. "Is this some sort of test for Ryan?"

She sighed as though he was wasting her time with all the questions.

Aunt Myra cleared her throat and told him without saying a word to not argue with his grandmother.

"I'm not trying to be difficult," Trevor said, "and I didn't even say I wouldn't come. I'm just honestly trying to understand why you're asking for my presence."

"Moral support," Grandma May said.

Grandpa and his friends broke into a round of boisterous laughter. It didn't have anything to do with Grandma's statement. Trevor still thought it was appropriate. Ryan had been getting more and more excited all weekend and more and more sure he didn't need to shadow anyone to know he wanted the job.

"He's not –"

Aunt Myra cleared her throat again before he could finish the sentence.

Grandma May raised her eyebrows in warning at the same time.

"I'm not arguing," Trevor said. "I'm only trying to reassure you that Ryan isn't nervous."

"Not about the job."

"Hey, May," Grandpa called, "Fred's grandson – the ten-year-old – has been trying to beat him at arm wrestling."

She gave half a smile. "You let him win yet?"

Fred shook his head proudly. It wasn't pride at besting a ten-year-old but that the kid wasn't giving up, and maybe that he'd challenged him in the first place.

Grandma May turned back to Trevor and picked up where she left off. "I know you and Audra have said you don't mind him taking over but being here would *show* him."

It would not have been arguing. Trevor would have pointed out that Ryan didn't need to see anything only to save her from worrying about something that didn't need any worry. Both women seemed to sense he was about to not argue though.

His grandma held up a finger and his great aunt said, "It would make your grandmother happy."

"I'll be back at noon," Trevor said. Anything else might have implied he didn't care if his grandmother was happy. He didn't need more coffee to know it was time to stop arguing.

16

It had been a slow morning, and Alison's mom had just returned from the back room with her second cup of coffee. She always had exactly two. Some days she spent so much time chatting with customers that she ran back to the microwave to reheat one or both several times before she could finish them. This was a day they were going fast. She stopped near Alison and held the familiar white mug to her lips. She seemed to only drink steam before she said, "It's quiet today."

Alison nodded.

Her mom looked towards the front window and back. "Not even Mary today."

Mary was a 90-year-old woman who had been a friend of Alison's grandmother. She took walks around town most mornings and sometimes stopped in to say hello. She had been in recently so it wasn't worrying that she hadn't stopped by that day. Alison acknowledged that the absence did add to the quiet feel. Her dad hadn't even been running any power tools.

"That's ugly."

"I know," Alison said, laughing a bit. She was painting another army green vine. The customer had raved about her previous work and asked about bringing in a set of chairs to have Alison copy the vine onto the seats. "I'm still trying to decide how to feel about having a talent for making ugly things."

"You're making it beautiful to someone."

"Yeah, I guess." She focused on the paper she was copying, trying to see the beauty in the drab colors. "It is unique," she conceded. "Even if it's not my taste, I can appreciate someone wanting what really appeals to... I mean, this is clearly someone who isn't just trying to jump on a trend."

Her mom sipped the coffee with agreement in her eyes. "Speaking of unique," she said, "how about I get those cards Audra gave me? I know it's not a real game when we each play two hands, but I think it's still helping me get the idea."

Alison frowned at this suspicious segue. There was a chance that rotting vines honestly reminded her mom of the special 56-card deck. It was possible that Alison didn't see the connection only because she'd become alert to suspicious segues.

Audra had approached them after church the previous day. She'd introduced them to Violet and explained that she'd gotten her excited about a regular Tichu game so now they had to do it and asked Alison's mom if she could be the fourth player. But there had been something off about the exchange, something that almost felt rehearsed. Alison had nearly convinced herself she was imagining things when Audra suggested she knew someone who could help if she turned out to be a bad teacher. A knowing look passed between her and Alison's mom when she said it. Alison asked if she meant Trevor. The question caused both of the others – and Violet, too – to smile as though she had stepped into a trap.

The whole thing had been weird. And then Audra pulled a deck of cards from her bag as soon as Alison's mom mentioned she'd prefer to practice before getting together as a group. Once they were alone – Alison's dad had made a beeline for the car as soon as it looked like socializing might happen – Alison asked her mom if she and Audra were up to something. The answer had been evasive, asking why she thought that rather than saying anything about her being crazy for thinking it.

Alison hadn't pushed at the time. Later in the day, however, when she'd started going over the rules she read, her mom brought up Trevor a few times. That wouldn't have been odd since she'd been bringing him up regularly for weeks except that she seemed to be looking for specific information. How would Alison react if she saw him somewhere other than their shop? Would she take advantage of such an opportunity? Alison had asked her mom point blank if she was involved in orchestrating such an opportunity, perhaps through a card game?

She never got a straight answer, which proved to Alison that there was a plan to get her and Trevor together through the game. And now her mom was smiling oddly as she brought up Tichu again. Regardless of ulterior motives, Alison was ready for a break from the vines.

"Okay," she said.

Her mom dealt out four hands on a nearby table while Alison cleaned up. She tried to focus on learning the game, but curiosity was churning up a lot of distraction. On the one hand, if people were plotting to get her and Trevor some time together, she wouldn't mind being set up as long as he could tell she'd been set up. The best way to not be in on it was to not ask too many questions. On the other hand, she was worried about it going badly.

They were expected at Audra's apartment on Friday evening. Trevor lived next door. What if this plan involved barging into his place where she might be unwelcome? He'd seemed completely uninterested in talking to Alison the last time she saw him. She could hardly look like an innocent bystander walking into his place when she knew it was his place, especially when she'd never explained how she'd just happened to know that.

Alison thought they followed all the rules on the first round, but it was hard to be sure without more experienced players around to correct them. She commented on as much.

"Yes," her mom agreed. "It's too bad Trevor isn't here to point out our mistakes."

"You mean Audra," Alison said. "She's the one teaching us."

"I guess." She shuffled slowly. "But you'd like to see Trevor again, right?"

Alison snapped. "All right, Mom. Just tell me what the plan is."

"Plan? What plan?" She didn't sound innocent or clueless.

"Come on. I can tell you and Audra are up to something."

"Well, I don't know how you've come to that conclusion, but tell me how you'd feel about it if we were."

"I'd want to know the plan."

Her mom chuckled and set the cards down. "Alison, honey, I just... Ever since he first walked in here, I've had this feeling that he's the one for you. I feel like this is what God wants. But I want to know if you feel it, too."

Alison shook her head. There was something unexplainable in her attraction to Trevor. She wasn't ready to label it God's will for her. "It doesn't matter anyway if *he* doesn't think so."

"Trevor? Why do you doubt his interest? It's obvious that he likes you."

"No, it isn't," Alison said. "I told you how fast he left on Saturday."

"And I told *you* that was because he didn't get enough signals from you."

"Mom..." Alison sounded a little whiny. She tried to even her tone before continuing. "I told him he could call me. I invited him to watch me work. I'm sure I looked thrilled to see him whether I was trying to or not."

Her mom smiled patiently. "You gave him your business card in a business setting. You invited him to watch *his* table. And... there's no two by four in there. Sometimes guys need a two by four to the head."

Alison laughed at the analogy even though she disagreed that she hadn't done just that.

"It's not their fault," her mom continued, "and it's not ours. But sometimes it really is like we're speaking different languages. When two people are speaking different languages, you gotta try harder to be sure you're getting your point across."

"So... you're scheming to give me a chance to bash him in the head?"

A playfully wicked expression appeared on her face at the accusation. "No one is scheming," she said. "If you happen to find yourself in a room with him, I might not have had anything to do with it."

Alison rolled her eyes. She might be calling it something else, but she was pretty sure her mom was scheming. It made her laugh though. Ever since Trevor had called her creepy, her mom seemed to be trying to turn the word into a compliment. She wasn't entirely failing either.

The two women started to focus on their Tichu practice about the time customers began to trickle into the shop. Alison went back to her painting whenever her mom needed to help someone and she didn't. With the interruptions, she hadn't made much progress on her work or her game by lunchtime. She was also still wondering what was being plotted or planned for Friday when her mom suggested she head next door for something to eat.

"Do you want me to bring you back something?"

"No, thanks. Your dad and I will take care of ourselves. You can eat over there if you want to give us some alone time."

Though she was never tired of the shop, Alison found the idea of a change of scenery surprisingly appealing. "Okay," she said. "I'll be back in a while."

Her mom waved, then scurried towards the back, presumably to make a lunch plan with her husband.

Alison stepped outside and found Audra standing on the sidewalk in front of the restaurant next door. She remembered that she'd said her grandparents owned it and wondered if she'd seen her there before she would have recognized her. It was a nice coincidence regardless.

"Alison! Perfect timing." Audra stuffed her phone in her pocket and pointed at the door. "Are you coming here to eat?"

"Yes, I am."

"Yay!" Audra pulled the door open and gestured for Alison to go in first. Then her mouth moved faster than her feet as they entered. "You can eat with us. This'll be great. Ryan is here. He's taking over as manager, and Grandma wanted me and Trevor to come in as a show of support. You know, to prove we're not upset that no one handed us a job. Because why would anyone be bothered by that?"

The bitter note may have been a joke because it dissolved completely into a smile and wave at a familiar woman Alison now guessed was Audra's grandmother. She had gray hair pulled back in a short braid. The place was busy and the older woman paused in wiping down one of the few empty tables to greet Audra. "Hello to my favorite grandchild," she said. "You brought a friend?"

"This is Alison Brachy," Audra said. "She works next door."

"Oh, right. Elaine's daughter."

Alison nodded. "Yeah. We've eaten here before. It's always good."

"Thank you. You're so sweet." She swiped her rag over the seat of the booth. "You girls can have this table, and I'll send Ryan out to wait on you."

There were menus at the table. Alison grabbed one but wasn't surprised that Audra didn't. They chatted about some of Audra's favorite dishes and some things Alison had tried. It had seemed only a minute before Audra's hand shot into the air in a wave. Alison glanced over her shoulder and saw that she was waving Trevor over to join them.

Alison should have expected him. In her welcome speech, Audra had said her grandmother asked her *and* Trevor, that Alison could eat with *us*. She had kind of buried it in a few other words though. Alison didn't know how nervous to feel. She could tell Trevor was surprised to see her, but she didn't even want to try to guess if it was a good surprise or a bad surprise.

"Have a seat," Audra said as he arrived at the table. She was looking at Alison's side and didn't budge from the edge of hers.

Alison slid over to make room for him.

Trevor had barely said hello to them when Ryan showed up at the table. "Hello," he said. "Is this your first time at the January Café?"

Audra rolled her eyes. "Shouldn't you be wearing a tie or something?"

"Why would I be wearing a tie?" Ryan asked. He was wearing a dark green polo shirt under a black apron. It was a nice color on him, though Alison probably wouldn't have noticed if Audra hadn't drawn attention to it. Trevor also had on a polo shirt, sky blue. She noticed that looked good without any help.

"To show that you're in charge," Audra said.

Ryan wrinkled his eyes. It seemed he wasn't entirely sure if she was kidding. "I'm not actually in charge yet, and Matt doesn't wear a tie. He wears a nametag that says 'manager.' That should be enough for me, too."

"If you say so." Audra sighed. "I'll have a glass of water, please."

Ryan looked expectantly at Alison.

She and Trevor both asked for water as well.

As Ryan left, Audra folded her hands on the table and said, "This is fun." Her eyes flit between Alison and Trevor for a moment. "So I hear Trevor gets his new and improved table on Thursday, just in time for the game on Friday. You might not see me this week because I'll be having my own game."

Trevor nodded. "I think we'll manage to suffer through the disappointment."

"Maybe." Audra wiggled her eyebrows at Alison as though they knew something he didn't. More confirmation that something was planned for Friday. It also felt like a hint to join the conversation.

"Audra's teaching me to play," she said.

"That's cool," he said. "I hope you like it."

"And my mom, too," she added.

Trevor stiffened as he nodded. He seemed to be making a point of keeping his mouth shut.

She didn't get a chance to ask if something was wrong before Audra's hand started waving towards the front door again. Was more family coming? Alison couldn't see around the back of the booth now that she was farther in.

"Hey, Logan." Trevor greeted the newcomer. He looked about the same age, and Trevor had mentioned that name as one of his friends, but he sounded confused to see him.

"Trevor." There was some surprise in Logan's voice as well as a big smile as he said, "Hi, Alison."

Now she was confused. She thought she recognized him from church but knew they'd never been introduced. She simply nodded to accept the greeting.

Audra jumped up and hooked her arm through Logan's. "Come with me a second," she said, practically dragging him away.

Alison stared at the back of Trevor's head as he watched them leave.

Ryan set three glasses of water on the table and looked where they were looking. "Uh... is Audra sitting over there now?"

She had pulled Logan to a nearby table for two, apparently intending to stay more than a second.

"I have no idea what Audra is doing," Trevor said.

"Neither does Logan," Ryan mumbled. He shook his head like he pitied the guy. Then he picked up one of the glasses and took it to her.

There was plenty of background noise in the crowded restaurant and nothing but silence in her particular booth as Alison pretended to read the menu. Everything had happened so fast she couldn't be sure, but she was beginning to think the card game had been a red herring. Was this the real plan her mom had concocted with Audra? It seemed that Logan would have had to be involved, and the grandmother in order to get Trevor here. Unless they knew she'd already asked him to come. It was awfully convenient that she was suddenly sitting alone with Trevor, but it was also somewhat embarrassing to think of how many people might have been involved. She was thoroughly hemmed in by his presence and yet felt more cozy than trapped. The silence had to be getting to him, too.

"Do you, uh…" He pointed to where Audra had been sitting. "Do you want me to move over there?"

"Do you think she's coming back?"

He shrugged. For a moment, he wore the same helpless expression as when he'd first asked her for coffee. There was something lost and vulnerable that made her want him to stay right where he was. Close. But it would be easier to talk facing each other, and less awkward.

"Um… whatever you want," she said.

Trevor slid from one side of the booth to the other and began to twist his water glass in a circle on the table.

Alison's side of the booth got a few degrees cooler from the absence. Her head was clearer though. He hadn't left the table. This could be an opportunity. There was enough tension that she was pretty sure he was only sticking around to be polite. But maybe not. If her mom was right, a little friendly conversation might help Alison determine if Trevor would be receptive to being clubbed upside the head. Figuratively, of course.

Ryan came back to take their orders so they were having lunch together. Alison intended to pay attention to how fast he ate and whether or not he was in a hurry to return to work.

17

She hadn't left. Trevor was overwhelmed by the turn of events. He'd expected Alison to get up to join Audra as soon as he cleared the way for her. But she'd stayed right there and even put in an order as though she didn't mind eating with him.

Hadn't she come in with Audra? Was she upset at having her company traded for Logan's or... Now that Trevor thought about it, it was kind of convenient that Logan had appeared when he had. Was this all planned? And was Alison in on the plan? Because that would mean he hadn't completely screwed up his chance with her after all.

"I have lunch here, um, I wouldn't say regularly," Alison said, "but often enough that I'm wondering if I've seen you here before."

"Probably not," he said. He glanced over his shoulder and lowered his voice. "My grandparents insist that family eats for free, and I don't want to take advantage. But it's tricky because I also don't want to look like I don't like it here. I usually just stop in for my morning coffee, and that seems to work for everyone."

"You get free coffee here?" Alison asked. "How did you end up looking for some at our place?" She nodded towards that side of the building.

"Oh, um... Grandma ran out. I was too groggy to realize how rude it was to stumble in begging you for some."

"It wasn't rude. It was –" Alison bit her lip as she cut herself off, presumably from saying something worse than rude. "How did a restaurant... I mean, it wouldn't take very long to make some more."

"There was some sort of problem with the coffee maker," he said. He was almost as eager to move away from memories of his terrible first and second impressions as he was to find out if Alison had expected to end up eating with him. "I hope you're not too upset that Audra ditched you."

Alison turned to Audra, who waved and smiled brightly, before she answered. "What do you mean?" she asked.

"Weren't you guys planning to have lunch together?"

"Oh, not..." Alison shrugged. "We just happened to come in at the same time. She didn't... Who's Logan?"

"Friend of the family," he said, trying not to show disappointment that Alison hadn't planned anything. She did still stay.

"I mean, who is he to Audra?"

"Just a friend as far as I know and as far as I want to know."

Alison smiled. She seemed amused that he didn't want to talk about his sister and who she was or was not dating. Her smile made him want to keep talking about what he didn't want to talk about to see if he could keep it around. But he honestly had nothing to say on the subject and staring at Alison wasn't filling his head with intelligent thoughts, only obvious statements about how pretty she was.

"So... Ryan is taking over this place?" she asked.

"Probably." He nodded to shake himself out of his stupor. "He hasn't officially taken the job. Today is sort of a trial, but I'd be very surprised if it doesn't happen."

She accepted what he said with a quick dip of her chin, then reached for her water.

"Are you, um…" Trevor wanted to ask if she had plans to take over the business next door now that he knew it was a family business. He hated to bring up her family though, especially when she didn't seem mad at him. Bringing up family was sure to remind her what he'd said about her mom.

Then again, whether she was mad or not, he felt he should apologize. That was probably the only way to keep from being awkward every time her mom came up. He really hoped to spend enough time with Alison that they couldn't avoid it so… "Alison, I want to say that I'm sorry if I offended you or your mom when I called her unhinged because I didn't know. It's not a good excuse since you tried to tell me, but things make more sense now, and I'm sorry."

Alison tilted her head and narrowed her eyes as he spoke. She wasn't looking at him in anger. It was more like bewilderment. "I remember creepy," she said. "When did you use the word unhinged?"

"Just before I left last Saturday. I told you about that maniacal laughter about… and then your dad came out and asked about your mom and started talking to her and I realized you hadn't been kidding when you said… uh… you don't remember that?"

"Oh. I do remember you saying she was laughing at me. And then my parents started yelling at each other across the shop about dinner plans, and I was shocked to see how late it had gotten." Her eyes had a faraway look as she brought the details to mind.

Trevor was panicking. She wasn't mad at him because she hadn't heard him. And now he'd gone and repeated it. He could not catch a break where Alison was concerned. He was doomed to screw up again and again and again.

Ryan brought the food.

"That was fast," Alison said.

He set a plate of lasagna in front of Trevor and a salad in front of Alison. It was a hearty salad topped with ham and eggs and cheese.

155

She looked at it approvingly while she thanked Ryan, and he left again.

Alison picked up her fork and poked around at the salad while Trevor waited for the conversation to catch up to her. And by some miracle, she laughed. "Unhinged?" she said. "I probably shouldn't tell my mom about that one." She set down her fork. "I told her how you said she was being creepy that first day, and she's totally running with it. Sometimes when it's just the two of us, she'll spy on me from around some big piece of furniture just to see how long it takes me to notice and then we both laugh."

Trevor said nothing. Was there another shoe here? Or was she actually letting him off the hook for all the stupid things he'd said?

She took a bite and chewed slowly, looking thoughtful. She swallowed. "I know you didn't mean anything. And I know my mom had been acting… because she, um…"

There was evidently something Alison wasn't sure she wanted to explain. Trevor wasn't going to ask. He was curious, but since it had to do with her mom he was going to steer clear for now. "Now that I know it's a family business…" He paused to make sure it was okay to ask a new question.

"And you won't get away with as much now that you know," Alison said sharply before she gestured for him to continue.

The warning finally let him relax. It was a solid boundary he had no fear of crossing. Now that he knew. "Do you have plans to take over someday?" he asked. "Not that your parents seem too near retiring or anything."

She nodded, finished chewing the bite she took while he was talking. "Eventually," she said, letting the word hang for a moment. "We all know the plan is for it to be mine someday, but I'm not in a hurry. I really don't want to run it by myself. I mean, I *couldn't* do it alone, and it would be hard to find people I trust as much as family based only on resumés."

Trevor understood the sentiment. There were plenty of good people in the world of course, but finding them wasn't always easy. He imagined his grandparents thinking along the same lines when they decided to ask Ryan about replacing Matt. "What about your sisters?" he asked.

"They're happy to let me have it," Alison said with a sigh. "Sometimes I try to think it's good we don't have to figure out how to share it, but mostly I think we could have made a good team. They both worked at the shop some in high school. But only cleaning and working with customers. They never had any interest in learning how to restore furniture." A smile lit up her face, apparently in response to a sudden memory. "My dad wanted to teach someone so badly that by the time I came along, I think I was going to be his apprentice whether I liked it or not. We were both lucky I had a genuine desire to learn."

"Sounds like it," Trevor said.

"Of course, my mom would say luck had nothing to do with it. She'd say it was part of God's plan to give my dad two daughters who rebuked his efforts so he'd appreciate the third more."

He had to ask about the dismissive tone. As much as he liked Alison, he couldn't get involved with someone who might laugh at the God stuff. Faith was too important to him. But he also didn't want to dive deep over a casual lunch. He tried to phrase the question lightly. "Did God not help you feel appreciated when you were being taught to sand whether you liked it or not?"

Alison smiled in a way that suggested she knew he wasn't talking exclusively about sanding. "I'm not saying she's necessarily wrong. I'm only saying she brings it up too often. Her favorite verse is the one somewhere in Romans about God uses everything for good for those who love him, or something like that. She's constantly asking where's the good in this or what good do you think God can make from this? I guess it's her way of looking for gratitude, of finding things to be grateful for. In my mature moments, I know

I should probably be trying to emulate that. But in other moments, I'm like, 'Again, Mom?'" She wrinkled her nose in an expression that wasn't exactly mature. It was very attractive though.

Talking to Alison fully awake allowed Trevor to stamp that expression into his memory to appreciate more later. It also gave him the sense to form his next question carefully. He wanted to ask about the name of her store and had a vague idea that he'd already mentioned it poorly at least once. "I've wondered about the name. Next Love? It's a fine name, but it doesn't say furniture to me. Is the next, like, because the furniture is looking for a second home or something?"

"Sort of." Alison took a sip of water. Trevor noticed that her salad was gone. "My grandma told me once that they wanted it to be a place where… after a piece of beloved furniture got so old and broken it just couldn't be used anymore, people could come in and find the next piece to love. And at the same time, pieces that people got rid of too quickly could find the next person to love them." She shrugged and rolled her eyes. "All that was way too much to put on a storefront so they picked the most important words and hoped everything in the window would fill in the blanks. If I think about it too much, I think love is too strong a word for furniture. But I don't think about it much because it's just always been the name."

"So you wouldn't change it if you took over?"

She shook her head. "We get a surprising amount of repeat business for… How often do people need furniture, you know? But a lot of people say, I got this here a few years ago and thought to look here now that I need this other thing. Or something like that. If I changed the name, people would probably think it was a new business, and I'd destroy a lot of… clout."

"What if that wasn't a concern?" Trevor asked. "If you could have picked the name, what would you have called it?"

Alison took a deep breath and blew it out slowly as she thought. "I don't know," she said after a minute. "I haven't given any thought to renaming something that already has a name, and that's something that would need some thought."

"Do you know why this place is called the January Café?"

She looked at him like it was a trick question and guessed, "Because it backs up to January Street?"

"That's what most people think," he said. "But that's only partly right."

"Really?" She sounded interested.

Trevor felt a pinch of ego at her tone. If it was up to him, they'd spend the whole time talking about her. She'd grow bored quickly if he didn't have anything to contribute though. "My grandparents are funny when they talk about it. Apparently, Grandpa wanted to name it after Grandma May. I think he wanted to name it May's Kitchen. But she hated the idea. She was like, 'I don't want my name on the window, you fool.' That's what she says when she tells the story. So he got the idea that since as you say it backs up to January Street, they could use January in the name as a code for Grandma's name since they're both months. Whenever he explains that, she gets all in a huff like it's the stupidest thing she's ever heard. She'll say, 'They're two different words. One is not code for the other.' And he'll say, 'In my mind, this place has always been named after you.' And she'll usually say something like, 'In your mind, things don't make a heap of sense.'"

Alison was cracking up at his impressions. That made them awesome no matter how accurate they were. She glanced around as she stopped laughing. Her gaze bounced across both of their empty plates so he figured out what she was looking for.

"I doubt he's coming back," he said.

"What?"

"Are you looking for Ryan?"

She nodded uncertainly, which counted as more interest.

"Grandma May won't let you pay because you're with me," Trevor explained. "I'm guessing Ryan is letting me tell you that rather than deal with the awkwardness of insisting it's on the house."

"Oh." She appeared to be processing how to deal with the awkwardness.

Trevor realized that as soon as she did, she would decide it was time to leave. He needed to make some sort of move. Clearly, she could tolerate his company. But was this meal about the same to her as one with Audra would have been? Or should he dare to hope for something more? The first thought that came to him was to suggest they do this again. Cliché but straightforward and expected. Except that "this" was not a date. It was a happy coincidence. That made the situation a bit more complicated. At least it did until Trevor admitted to himself that it wasn't semantics but a sad lack of courage that was stopping him.

"I guess the next time I'll see you will be Thursday," he said. That was when she was going to deliver his table. He was praying that it would mean something to her that he said the *next* time and not the *last* time. Not only was changing one word about the wimpiest move he could have made, he was afraid he was being a little like his grandpa in thinking something that made sense in his head would be obvious to the rest of the world.

Alison only gave a brief nod of confirmation.

"And is that... Do you have other deliveries that night?" That question felt bolder. Surely it hinted that he was curious about her time and wanting to suggest ways she could spend it with him.

"No," she said. "And even if something came up, I could always schedule you last."

Trevor had been nervously drumming his fingers on the table. He hadn't even known he was doing it until Alison put her hand on top of his. It wasn't her whole hand. She only brushed her fingers along the backs of his as if to settle them. But it was like a ton of bricks falling on his head with the announcement that she was giving him permission to hope. "You'd have time to stick around then and... make sure I get the table installed properly?"

She chuckled at his lame joke. Amazing. "As long as you're willing to help me get it off the truck," she said, "because otherwise I'll have to bring my dad."

"Absolutely." He nodded eagerly. "Ryan will be there, too, so even if I happen to break my arm between now and then, we'll be good."

She was still smiling. "You really think there's a chance you're going to break your arm in the next three days?"

Trevor shrugged. He was making plans with a beautiful woman he'd repeatedly insulted and acted like a moron around. At the moment, there was nothing he would declare impossible.

"Okay, well, I really should get back to work," she said as she slid from the booth. "Thank your grandma for lunch for me and, uh, I'll see you soon."

He nodded and waved. He watched her leave, basking in a moment of gratitude that took zero effort. Was he ever glad he agreed to make his grandmother happy. A check of the time told him he needed to get back to work, too. He jumped up and rushed to the door.

"Getting dressed up for a delivery, huh?"

If she was expecting some sort of withering look, she would be disappointed. Alison responded matter-of-factly. "I put on a clean shirt, Mom. That does not constitute dressing up."

"You look nice in red."

"Thank you," Alison said. She had chosen that shirt because she never wore it to work so it was one of the few casual tops in her closet that didn't have any stains. She had stopped at home to change before the delivery because she'd used her shirt as a rag one too many times that day. She didn't mind being messy at work. It gave credence to the assertions that the woodworking happened on site, maybe even made her look capable. Trevor had already seen her looking capable. Now she wanted him to see her looking clean. Or at least cleaner. All of her jeans had at least a few paint spots.

"Are you sure you won't need my help?" Alison's dad was sitting in a comfy chair about to remove his shoes.

"I think the four of us can handle it, Dad." It wasn't a very big table, and she knew she could carry it herself if it came to that so he deserved the sarcastic tone.

He ignored the tone and even appeared to seriously consider the merits of her statement before he said, "Those boys better not make you and Audra help."

Alison only chuckled as though he might be kidding, though she was pretty sure he wasn't.

"I could find out," her mom volunteered. "I could follow you and drive around the block a few times while you unload. It would keep up my persona."

Alison was sure that was a joke, but she still said, "Please don't."

Her mom laughed before she dropped the act. "Have a good time. We won't wait up for you."

"Speak for yourself." Her dad had already pushed back the recliner and closed his eyes.

"Good night," Alison said. She grabbed her keys and left the two most annoying people she loved.

She drove to the Founder's Mansion feeling almost like she was going to a party. Aside from occasional visits with her sisters, which included babysitting half the time, she didn't leave herself much time for a social life. The planning probably added to the party feel.

Trevor had texted her a few hours after they met for lunch asking if he should get a pizza for Thursday. She agreed. Audra texted next to ask if she could come. She'd said that since Ryan would be there, she'd actually be a fourth wheel, which was the best number for games.

Audra then informed Trevor in a group text that Ryan and Alison had already said she could come and started a discussion of which game they should play. This was mostly Audra listing games to which Ryan or Trevor replied negatively before Alison even saw the suggestion. She apparently had a lot of games her brothers didn't like. Maybe that was why Tichu had become so popular in their family. It was the only game they could agree on.

Audra was standing outside when Alison parked. Alison waved before she got out of the truck.

"Hi!" Audra said. She walked right up to the curb.

Alison looked at the table in the back, wondering if maybe with Audra right there they shouldn't just get it now rather than come back for it.

Audra interpreted her hesitation. "We'll let the guys get it," she said.

"But we're right here."

"Trust me." Audra motioned towards the house, and Alison began walking with her. "They'll be mad if we unload it. Picking up heavy things is one of the ways guys prove they're useful."

"It's not that heavy," Alison said.

"It's still big." Audra grinned. "This'll be fun. I bet the door's unlocked."

"Uh…" Alison looked uncertainly at the door they were quickly approaching. Were they just going to walk in?

"Trevor always leaves the door unlocked when he thinks I'm coming over," Audra explained. "That way, he doesn't have to get up to let me in, and he can give me a hard time about not making him get up to let me in. I want to see what he says if you're with me."

Alison didn't have a chance to question the appropriateness or the logic before Audra pressed the doorbell and was inside while it was still ringing. Alison stayed a step behind, taking her time to close the door behind them. She turned around and saw Trevor shaking his head at Audra.

"You're not going to say anything today?" she asked, glancing back at Alison.

"Why bother?" he said. "You already know that's not how it works." He smiled to welcome Alison as his sister took a few quick steps past him towards her painting on the wall.

Alison said, "Hello," to Trevor but kept her eyes on Audra, who was taking something from her pocket. It turned out to be a tiny level. She set it on top of the frame.

Ryan entered the room from a doorway off to the side. He saw what Audra was doing and made an exaggerated eye roll.

"Again?" he said. "No one has touched it since you were here last time."

"You don't know that," Audra said, though she put away the level without adjusting the painting.

"I live here," Ryan said.

"Exactly." Audra waved a hand between her brothers. "With both of you clodhoppers bumping into walls and stuff, it's a wonder the painting even stays on the wall."

"How clumsy do you think I am?" Ryan asked.

Was that what clodhopper meant? Alison smiled as she thought she really had created a monster, a kind of funny one.

"Pizza will be here in a few minutes," Trevor said. "We should probably get the table inside first." His eyes found Alison's for instructions.

"Okay." Alison gladly led them back outside because she couldn't fully relax until she finished her job.

She hopped onto the back of her truck and unfastened the straps holding the table. Trevor and Ryan climbed up behind her and positioned themselves on either end of it. It was obvious they intended to pick it up without help, though Alison did offer some advice on getting it off the back without damaging it. She slammed the tailgate and easily caught up to the slow pace set by guys awkwardly joined by a table. Neither appeared to struggle with the weight.

"Do you and your dad do all the deliveries yourselves?" Trevor asked. There was an interesting tenor to the question. It sounded as though he was halfway between impressed and outraged by the idea.

It made sense for him to wonder though. While Alison and her dad managed to move everything within the shop, she knew there were plenty of large, solid objects they couldn't handle if there were steps involved, or anything else that required getting it more than an inch off the ground. "We contract most deliveries to a local company with muscle, but we do some smaller things ourselves when we can save money."

Trevor nodded. So did the other two listening.

Ryan must have remembered how he helped her dad get it outside because he tipped the legs through the doorway like he knew what he was doing. Soon it was in the kitchen. Trevor and Ryan put the chairs around it and stood there admiring it. At least, Alison hoped they were admiring it.

The doorbell rang.

"I'll get it," Ryan said.

Trevor got out some plates and napkins for the pizza.

"Plates *and* napkins?" Audra teased. "Fancy."

"We need to be careful of the..." Trevor stopped before he actually set the plates down. "Unless maybe we should use a tablecloth?"

Audra snorted. "Do you even own a tablecloth?"

"Yeah," he said. "Mom gave me one at some point. I'm just not sure, uh... where I put it."

Ryan returned holding two pizza boxes. He stopped as he sensed the hesitation in the room.

"It's a table, guys," Alison said. "It's okay to put stuff on it. Besides... if you mess it up, you can always hire me again."

Audra laughed and the guys made the food available. Some silence and crossing indicated they were offering similar prayers of thanks on their own as they claimed chairs. The pizza was delicious, not that anyone found that surprising.

Ryan and Alison reminisced about school a bit. He shared updates on a few classmates he kept in touch with, and she did the same. Though Trevor and Audra had been in different classes, they attended the same high school and had comparable memories. Alison enjoyed getting to know the three siblings better during the meal. She didn't feel at all out of place as she had separate connections to each of them. They had been talking over empty pizza boxes for a while when Trevor suggested they move on to a game.

"Did you decide on something?" Alison asked. She stood up to try to help while the guys cleaned the table.

Audra had moved to a shelf in the corner stacked high with flat colorful boxes. "Let's go classic tonight." She held up *Settlers of Catan.* "Do you know this one, Alison?"

"I think so," she said. "But ours looks different."

"It's the same game," Audra said, bringing it to the table. "We're just very classic because we have it in the original box."

"We?" Ryan raised his eyebrows at her.

"Okay. *Ryan* has it in the original box."

Trevor began to set up the board. Audra and Alison reached for the bag of white pieces at the same time.

"Oh." Alison's hand froze with uncertainty. She was happy to let Audra have it, but she didn't know anyone else's usual color either and didn't want to grab one of those next.

Audra plucked a die from the box. "I'll roll you for it," she said. "Loser gets yellow."

Alison agreed to the simple solution, though she ended up with yellow. Everyone seemed to think the board was unusually crowded as the starting placements were slowly established. It seemed they were finally ready to begin when Audra said, "By the way, Mom and Dad want to meet you."

Alison smiled at the expression that appeared on Trevor's face at this statement. He looked guilty, which she interpreted to mean he'd been talking about her. That was a thought that made her smile.

"No rush," he said. "However long it takes, they'll assume the delay is my fault."

"That's because we all assume everything is Trevor's fault," Audra quipped.

He knocked over her carefully constructed tower of roads and cities.

"Hey!" Audra began to rebuild it, smiling at what was apparently acceptable retaliation. "They also want to meet you to thank you for letting me hang my paintings. I picked out the ones I'll bring on Saturday."

"I guess you sort of have Grandma's broken coffee maker to thank for that, too." Trevor shared a knowing look with Alison. It suggested she didn't yet know how grateful he was that they'd met. Her face flushed, and she mashed her lips against an overly giddy smile.

"Which one?" Ryan asked.

Glances flit around the table as no one seemed to know whom he was addressing.

"Which one what?" Trevor asked.

"Which coffee maker was broken?" he said. "They have three back there."

"Ryan!" Audra sort of whisper-yelled his name.

"Ow!" And it seemed she'd stomped on his foot at the same time. "What did I do?"

"Just... nothing." Audra shoved the dice at him. "Let's play."

"Grandma has *three* coffee makers?" Trevor's question sounded more like a revelation.

Audra rolled her eyes. "You got Grandma in trouble. That's what you did."

"Oh, wait a minute." Ryan's eyes widened as he caught on, and he wasn't trying very hard not to laugh.

Alison figured it out as well. She was enjoying the emotions on Trevor's face too much to be upset or embarrassed herself. He kept sighing and glancing at Alison. He looked as though he wanted to yell at someone for having been tricked but couldn't escape the fact that he was glad he'd been tricked.

"Tell me what you know," he said to Audra, "and how long you've known it."

168

She smiled sweetly as she thought about it. "Well, I guess since – as Grandma would say – the cat's out of the bag, I might as well spill the rest of the beans. It sounds like she and Elaine – um, Alison's mom – have been talking about getting the two of you together for some time. One of the coffee makers really has been kind of flakey, and that's where she got the idea. She said she was nervous about sending you over there first thing in the morning when she knew you might not be at your best…"

Audra paused to let Trevor groan at the truth of that observation. "But she was afraid you'd be too smart to fall for anything later in the day. So they went with that plan. I didn't get involved – or know anything about it – until," she thought for a moment, then fixed Alison with an earnest expression, "about the same time I asked you to learn to play Tichu with me. But I want you to know I really want to get a game going. It's just that once Grandma told me they needed reinforcements because Trevor wasn't going to cooperate anymore because he did something stupid or something, and then I thought maybe we could use the Tichu to maybe get Trevor to come over and sub for Violet or something.

"I also thought about getting him to drop off some paintings for me, but that probably would have been too obvious. Then Grandma decided to keep it simple and tell Trevor to have lunch at the restaurant the same day Alison's mom suggested she eat there. All I had to do was get us at the same table and bring Logan in to give me an excuse to not eat with you two." She smiled with satisfaction at how simple the manipulation had been.

"Logan knew about this?" Trevor asked.

"No." Audra shrugged. "I mean, he does now. He thought something was fishy when I asked him to meet me at exactly 12:10, but he didn't realize what we were doing until he got there. I didn't tell him how Grandma orchestrated any previous meetings."

Alison was quietly processing this information, particularly her mother's part in it. She intended to get more information directly from her mom rather than have anyone there focus on it. Trevor might feel less remorse at his early assessments of her.

Ryan held up the dice. "Should we go ahead and play?"

"Yeah," Trevor said. He shook his head as though he would continue to be disgusted in silence. It was quickly forgotten as they got into the game though.

Most of the conversation revolved around friendly arguments about who was getting stolen from more often. Audra might have won that argument as it seemed her brothers teamed up against her. It wasn't enough to stop her from winning the game as well. It was a little past 9 PM by the time they were congratulating her. That wasn't late late, but Alison decided it was too late to suggest another game. They all had jobs the next day, and she didn't want to overstay her welcome.

Audra noticed her checking the time. "You thinking of heading home, Alison?"

She nodded and began to collect her pieces. "I should probably call it a night."

"Okay." Audra jumped up and moved towards the door. "I'll leave first so I'm not in the way when Trevor wants to walk you out."

Alison kept her eyes on the bag of yellow pieces rather than see what anyone thought of that comment.

"You can still help us put it away first," Ryan said.

"What?" Audra turned around looking playfully shocked. "Surely you'd be insulted if I suggested you needed help lifting all those tiny little pieces. Goodnight!" She sang the last word as she left.

Ryan looked amused despite himself. He swept Audra's pieces into a bag, and the game was back in the box in less than a minute. Ryan took it back to the shelf.

"Well, um, thanks for the food and the game, guys," Alison said, taking a small step towards the exit.

Ryan glanced back long enough to wave. "You're welcome."

Trevor took a step towards the door as well. "I... I suppose it would be rude not to walk you out after Audra pointed out it'd be a good idea."

"Okay." Alison allowed him to lead her outside. It seemed like a good idea partly because she thought he was a little embarrassed about it. He walked all the way down the sidewalk without saying anything and around the front of her truck.

She stopped by the driver's door but made no move to open it. If he wanted to come outside to say goodnight, she wanted to give him a minute.

"Alison, can I... can I ask you something?"

She nodded and swatted at a mosquito that had apparently been waiting for a meal.

"Can I see you again?"

"Yes," she said.

"That wasn't it."

Alison felt her eyes scrunch as he rushed to keep talking.

"I mean, I definitely want to see you again, but we don't have to make specific plans as long as you're okay with me calling you and..."

Alison nodded again as he trailed off. She lifted her heel to swat at her calf. That was a determined insect to bite through denim.

"What I wanted to ask," Trevor said, "is that I know I," he gestured to the house, "*everyone* knows I got off to a rocky start here and... Can you tell me what I did right so I can keep doing whatever that was?"

"I don't know," Alison said. The question was sweet though so she tried to fight through some nerves to answer honestly. "You got my attention, I guess. From the moment you couldn't figure out how to open the door, I started to wonder what your story was."

Trevor pinched his lips as though he was trying not to frown at her. "I think saying I couldn't figure out the door is going a bit far, and you gotta admit there's something weird about it. It's this big, extra wide slab of wood that's... Is it hollow or something?"

Alison shrugged. "I just know I've never seen anyone else have trouble with it."

"I thought you were going to tell me what I did *right*." He sighed visibly.

They shared a very brief laugh before he sobered and looked as though he still wanted an answer. Alison tried to figure out how to say that he was cute when he was a bumbling idiot without using the exact words. "Well... you came in asking for coffee and dismissed my work as junk."

Trevor opened his mouth to cut her off.

"*But*," she continued, "there was this look in your eyes like you were on a runaway train or something. I was sure you were trying to be nice. Somehow."

"Trying is the key, huh?" He seemed to be considering whether or not that was something he could handle. His hand came up and rested on the side mirror of her truck, which made him seem suddenly closer. Unless he was also leaning forward, and it wasn't an illusion. He was close enough to kiss her.

Alison felt a teeny tiny stab on her forearm. She ignored it to avoid breaking the moment. They both knew this was the reason he came outside with her. A streetlight was reflected in the blue part of his eyes. She tried to think about how mundane a streetlight was and not how those eyes fluttered between her eyes and her mouth. She was too aware of her lips and couldn't move them or keep them still without being self-conscious.

Trevor moved back. He wasn't going to rush it. "I probably won't see you tomorrow even though you'll be next door."

She nodded regretfully and slapped her arm. The bugs were going to eat her alive if she waited around for something she hoped would have many more opportunities to happen. "I will see you soon though. Goodnight." She opened the door and jumped inside.

He walked around the front of the truck and waved as she drove away.

19

*A*lison's mom noticed her scratching a bite on her arm. "How long were you outside last night?"

"Too long and not long enough," Alison said.

A confused expression was her only response.

"And that's all I'm saying."

"Hmm. Cryptic." Her mom took a sip of her coffee with a thoughtfully amused look on her face.

"That's really it," Alison insisted. Her parents hadn't been asleep when she got home, but they had been in their bedroom watching TV. They hadn't asked anything over breakfast beyond whether or not she'd had fun. And they were focused on talking shop as they arrived. The three of them went over who planned to accomplish what during the day. That sort of occasional recapping of goals was as close as they came to having staff meetings.

Alison had expected questions from her mom once they were alone. She'd started the day with a little banging and power tools at her dad's side. When she was ready for a break, she found she was also ready for the questions. After all, she had a few of her own.

"Since you seem happy, can I assume you'll be spending more time with Trevor in the future?"

"That's a safe bet," Alison said. "Although the most interesting part of the evening was something Audra let slip about you."

Her mom frowned at her mug. "I need to warm this up."

"Not right now." They were standing on either side of a dresser, facing each other while leaning against it. Alison made a move to the side to block her mom's attempt to retreat. "I think we need to talk about you talking about me."

"What do you mean?"

"You know what I mean." Alison rolled her eyes at the false innocence. "How long have you and May over there been trying to play matchmaker? And when did you even... I mean, I'm with you a lot."

She propped her elbow on the top of the dresser again. Her mom spoke seriously, as though discussing some important research instead of her meddling. "I've known May forever, stopping in there for lunch before you were even born, though we weren't on a first name basis back then. I introduced all you girls to her when you started working with us, told her when Amanda and Angela got married and about my grandbabies. And we certainly don't talk only when you're around. She called me just this morning while you were in the back to let me know our cover had been blown. Apparently, she got a shockingly coherent earful from Trevor this morning."

Alison was beginning to wonder when all the backstory would begin to include the story she'd asked for.

"At some point, I lamented that you didn't seem to be in any hurry to get married."

That wasn't better than backstory, but Alison continued to listen.

"May brought up her eligible grandsons. We gave careful consideration before we made a move. We thought of Ryan first since he's the same age as you. But we decided that since you two were in school together that something would have already happened there if it was going to. She only has two others that wouldn't be too young for you, Trevor and a 23-year-old whose name I don't recall at the moment. The 23-year-old is apparently having a little trouble making an adult of himself, seems to be wasteful with money and a bit of a thrill-seeker. Sounds like a decent young man – or at least soon to be – but not a good match for you. Trevor, on the other hand, he's nice and responsible with a strong faith. He's not the sharpest tack first thing in the morning, but we thought that was something you could overlook. And we knew he'd like you, too. From my perspective of course, there's nothing not to like." The tongue-in-cheek statement was accompanied by a one-handed flourish like someone displaying a game show prize.

Alison sighed and waited for her mom to get serious again. She still hadn't gotten to the part where the two women decided to stage a meeting.

"May thought Trevor was looking for a smart girl who wasn't afraid to get her hands dirty. She didn't think he'd be into a frilly type. Obviously, it was a great idea to get you two together."

"Okay," Alison said. "If you really thought it would work out, why didn't you just introduce us to each other? Why the sneakiness?"

"We considered that," she said. "I thought I could probably talk you into a blind date, but that would have been a high-pressure situation. We thought it'd be easier on both of you if we let things happen naturally."

"Naturally?" Alison scoffed. "How many people were involved in tricking us into having lunch together this week?"

"Yes, well, that was only after things failed to go as smoothly as we hoped."

"Things might have gone smoother if you hadn't been skulking around to see if your plan was working."

Her mom smiled. She seemed to now think skulking was a positive verb. "Someday, when I'm Trevor's mother-in-law, we will all laugh at his perception of me. Provided he knows what's good for him."

"And what about all that talk about how a guardian angel sent him here because it was God's plan, when you knew all along that it was *your* plan?"

"Who do you think gave us the idea?"

"Go heat up your coffee, Mom. I'm going to see if there's anything I can use pliers on." Alison ignored the laughter as she went back to her work area. She actually had staining next on her list, but wanting to pinch and twist seemed like an apt description of her feelings.

She was really annoyed that she wasn't more annoyed. She should be very bothered that her mom had been arranging this behind her back and more so that she'd been right about her liking Trevor. Except that Alison did like him. It was difficult to be mad at the start of a promising relationship.

At least her mom didn't have much time to gloat. After their initial chat, the shop saw a steady stream of customers. Alison ducked into the back to eat a sandwich she'd brought from home. Then she avoided starting a project so she'd be more readily available for customers while her mom went out for her lunch. She didn't mention where she was going, and Alison didn't ask. She didn't want to think about who she might be talking to or about. She suspected gloating.

Dinner promised to be more relaxing. Audra didn't think they should eat pizza two nights in a row. She was making a dish with tilapia and rice while Alison's mom put together a salad to go with it. The four ladies had a very civilized meal where they tried to learn a bit more about each other.

Audra and Violet had been roommates their first year of college. It had been the only year for both of them, and they decided to get an apartment together the following year. Violet had one sister who was getting married in a few months.

Alison was paired with Violet for Tichu. She hadn't learned yet how competitive she was and was nervous about testing her patience with beginner mistakes. It was a friendly game though. Audra and Violet corrected Alison and her mom gently, trying to help them become better players and not just less annoying partners. The game ended in victory for Alison and Violet, though Alison was sure Violet had carried the team.

"Let's go check on the guys," Audra said. She jumped up while Violet was still getting the cards back in the box.

"I thought we were staying here tonight," Violet said.

"It's too early to call it a night and too late for another game, right?"

Violet shrugged.

Alison looked at her mom.

"I'm probably too old to play another game tonight," she said. "Need to save some energy for next week."

"Come on." Audra moved towards her door.

Alison followed because she knew "the guys" included Trevor. He'd texted that afternoon that he had an idea for an outing but wouldn't tell her what it was. She hoped to get the information in person.

"Wait one minute," Violet said. She slipped into her bedroom.

"It's still strange to me that your walls are bare," Alison commented. "It seems like an artist should be surrounded by art."

"I can't hang them all up, and I wouldn't know which ones to choose. Plus, I'm not a real artist."

"You are. And I'm glad you chose to share that talent with us." Alison's mom appeared thoughtful. "That's the good," she said. "When May and I decided to *lovingly* meddle, God used that to bring your art into the world."

"Wow." Audra's eyes got big. "It's a bit much to suggest my amateur paintings are any kind of inspirational tool."

"Good doesn't have to be earth-shattering."

Alison found herself agreeing with her mom. "Yeah, you know that song, *Dream Small?* Every good thing matters, even if it's just a picture to brighten someone's day."

Audra tipped her head, looking as though they were still attaching too much importance to her hobby but that she appreciated the thought regardless.

"Thanks for waiting," Violet said as she reappeared. She had tucked in the front of her shirt and repinned her hair so that more of the spirals cascaded around her face.

Audra led them around the building to Trevor's apartment and rang the doorbell four times before walking in.

Alison was right behind her so she heard Trevor say, "What in the world was that?"

"I was letting you know that four people were coming in." She grinned at him.

Logan put his head down to cover some of his amusement.

"That's really not how it works," Trevor said. "Hi, Alison."

"Hi, Violet," Ryan said.

Cameron silently waved at all of them.

"Everyone, this is Alison's mom, Elaine Brachy. You know Trevor and Ryan. That's Logan, and that's Cameron." Audra made the introductions while she walked around the table and picked up a phone. Judging by its position on the table and the way he watched her, it was Logan's. "Oh, you guys are close," she said. "You'll probably win after this hand."

"No, we won't," Trevor mumbled.

"Wasn't talking to you," Audra said.

"We can't win if no one's playing." Ryan gestured to the trick he'd led.

"I passed," Cameron said.

That made it Logan's turn. "Oh, uh… pass," he said.

Trevor also passed. The game ended a minute later. Alison knew they had started later so she was a little surprised. "You guys must play fast," she said.

"They keep it moving," Audra answered for them, not that an observation really needed an answer. "Probably time for another game."

There was some nodding around the table, and Logan was already shuffling the cards. Alison supposed the rounds would go faster when two of the players didn't have distractions in the room. Trevor wouldn't have time to talk. "I guess two of us can get out of your way." She met his eyes. "Do you want to tell me that idea first?"

"Um…" He seemed to take in the crowd of people in the room. "We can talk about it tomorrow."

"Just take him outside and get it out of him," Audra said. "These guys can wait five minutes." She winked at Alison's mom, who gave her daughter a light nudge on the arm.

It appeared people hadn't entirely finished their meddling, loving or otherwise.

Trevor stood up as though it wasn't a bad idea so Alison went ahead and followed him to the door. They were halfway out when her mom said, "You can signal me through the window when you're ready to go."

Alison groaned inwardly.

Trevor closed the door, then glanced back as the meaning caught up to him. He smiled faintly. The creepiness wasn't going to worry him anymore. Though he did position himself with his back to the nearest window.

"It's lame," he said, "but I just thought maybe on Sunday we could go to the zoo. It's supposed to be a little cooler, and it'd be an excuse to walk around with stuff to look at and talk about."

"I don't think I've been to the zoo since I was a kid," Alison said. "That might be fun."

"Good." He looked relieved. "You won't be done with church until after eleven. Do you want to plan on eating lunch before I pick you up?"

"Yeah, I should. Zoo food is probably really overpriced."

He nodded slowly.

Alison wasn't sure if he thought agreeing too vigorously would make him look cheap or if perhaps he was disappointed not to get in more time with her. That would be sweet, but if he really wanted a practical, no frills sort of woman... there was nothing cheap about not wanting to spend eight dollars on a hot dog.

"Okay... so about 1 o'clock?"

"12:30," she said, in case he did want more time.

Trevor smiled. "Sunday at 12:30. And you'll text me your address between now and then?"

"Or I could pick you up."

"Whatever," he said, still smiling. He could tell she was only teasing and not actually refusing to tell him where she lived. He moved closer, and the mosquitos weren't biting.

Alison felt her eyes flicker up and down his face, which she knew would look like an invitation.

He accepted. He leaned in and kissed her. It was quick, but enough to send some tingles all the way to her toes.

"I... I better get back to the game," Trevor said as he opened the door. "Goodnight."

She didn't mind his quick exit. She didn't need anyone inside imagining a goodbye that wasn't quick. "Time to go, Mom," she yelled through the open door. Alison knew she was nowhere near the window, but she was still glad to see it. Her feet were light on the way out knowing that she and Trevor were finally on secure footing. Though mixed in with the budding joy was an uneasy feeling that now it was Alison's turn to make mistakes. She supposed that meant it would be Trevor's turn to be forgiving. A good relationship could survive with equal amounts of mistakes and forgiveness. And maybe they didn't have to take turns.

~~ The End ~~

~~ Thank you for reading. ~~

www.ingramcontent.com/pod-product-compliance
Lightning Source LLC
Chambersburg PA
CBHW031348170626
46807CB00002B/879

* 9 7 8 1 9 4 3 5 9 8 1 4 4 *